Streaming James

Streaming Souls Psychic Detective Mystery Series

A Walk-In Investigations Paranormal Detective Novel

by Joyce Kostakis

Paperback edition Interacting Worlds Press

Edition Date: May 9, 2021

ISBN: paperback 978-1-7346673-2-5

ISBN: ebook 978-1-7346673-0-1

Library of Congress Control Number: 2021908118

Cover Image: Linda-AfterTenDesign

Book Patch LLC, The, Scottsdale, Arizona

Dedication

To my husband Michael for his continued encouragement and support.

To my favorite sister Evelyn. She is my only sister but, she knows that if we had another sister, she would still be my favorite. Her feedback and support kept the momentum going.

I didn't write this book alone. To the North Ridgeville Writers group that helped me polish the chapters, I can't thank you enough for your willingness to read and re-read as I revised the chapters based on your invaluable feedback. It's because of you that this book made it to its final form. To Susan Fox, her creative insights and meditation techniques for writing made the process fun and enjoyable. To Chelsea Piper, whose insights made the last chapters come together.

To my editor Nancy Naizer and all of my beta readers, I can't thank you enough for your feedback, support, and keen eye when reviewing the chapters.

Chapter 1

I flung the case file labeled 'James Baxter, March 3, 2037,' onto my desk in exasperation. I kicked my rolling chair across the room and looked back at the documents spilled across my desk. I was usually careful with the case documents, not only because they were brittle with age, but they belonged to Dad.

Dad hated electronic files. He refused to use any device for taking notes or storage. He claimed e-files were one power surge away from disappearing.

Six weeks of working on the James Baxter murder and I was no closer to solving it than Dad was twenty years ago. Endless nights of struggling to channel James with nothing to show for it but nagging doubts about my psychic abilities.

The frustration of not being able to connect with James made me want to slit my wrists. That's an exaggeration. My style was vodka and pills. If you can call a one-time event a 'style'. I'm never traveling down that road again. The paramedics revived me, but, crossing over, no matter how fleeting, changes you forever. It's because of my suicide attempt the door to the afterlife stayed wide open and I'm standing here staring at gruesome crime scene photos trying to hail the dead.

Before crossing over, my only battle was forging my path as a homicide detective which I did successfully for the past fifteen years, despite working in the shadow of my dad, the famous homicide detective, Jim Hanson. Dad still held the record for the fastest-rising detective. His closing ratio on solving homicide cases was rarely beat.

My name, Katie Hanson, often escaped the memory of my coworkers. They referred to me as Jim's daughter or mini-Jim.

You're so lucky to learn from Jim, they had said. Learn from him? Until I solved the Alexander triple murder, he barely acknowledged my existence.

Dad was charismatic and the focus of attention in almost every setting. When my twin brother Jimmy died at age ten, a part of me died with him. The pity in everyone's eyes at a twin living without her other half was a constant reminder of his death. Over time, it was more comfortable to be invisible than to be the center of attention.

Yes, I had Dad's integrity, gut instinct, and drive, but we diverged in our investigative styles. Yet the guys always compared us. For most of my career, Dad's stats loomed over me. But now I can stream the dead and close the department's cold cases in record time. At least that had been the plan until James put the kibosh on it by withholding his help.

The slaughter of James Baxter was one of Portland, Oregon's, most prominent cases. It wasn't the limelight that got me to volunteer for the case: more like a moment of weakness. As was customary when we closed a case, the captain set up a celebration at the pub after I solved the Alexander triple homicide. We were still celebrating when Dad showed up an hour into the festivities and asked if we could talk. My ego was still riding the high from using my new psychic skills to solve the death of Sarah Alexander and her two children, so I followed him to an open booth.

I'm sure the beers suppressed the memory of our estrangement, or perhaps it was the first time he looked at me with pride. Whatever the cause, after hearing Dad's story about the one case he never solved still haunting him all these years later, my ego bypassed my brain and promised to not only channel James Baxter, but solve the case before Dad's retirement party in a few months.

You can't blame me for assuming every soul would stand in line waiting for the chance to help lock away his or her killer. Channeling Sarah was so easy. With my first attempt, she came barreling in, adamant about how her murder went down, with no doubt in her mind who pulled the trigger and killed her.

There was no hesitation when she told me who had killed her and her children. She was front and center from the beginning. When I shared my doubts, she caused a painting to fly off my wall, missing my head by a hair's breadth. She ran the show.

After that, what medium wouldn't assume they could solve their cases in record time? I was so confident of this, I retired from the department and joined my best friend and mentor's psychic development group. Vicky offered me an empty office, and the use of her staff, which helped me start my Private-Third-Eye Detective Agency, Walk-In Investigations.

I already had my first client lined up. The captain from my former homicide department saw me channel Sarah and agreed to be a pilot site for what we hoped would be a nationwide partnership between homicide divisions across the nation. After dealing with Dad's case, I would make my way through the department's backlog. How was that going to play out with James running silent? Was this cold case not meant to be solved?

It had been a few weeks since Dad dropped off three boxes of his case files. Dad was counting on me and I had smugly boasted of solving the case. I couldn't give up. I had to stop procrastinating. Seeing my sweet Catahoula pup, Cooper, curled up in his bed next to my desk relaxed me. After a few deep breaths, I picked up a photo of James for another round and held it between my hands and closed my eyes.

"James? ... James Baxter, please share your story."

Nothing.

Automatic writing might work. I cleared a spot on my desk and turned on my virtual keyboard. The letters floated a few centimeters above my desk. Words flowed freely from my fingers about the facts of the case, but no new details came through. My hopes that his information would come through midstream were dashed. James was not cooperating at all.

I glanced at the contents of the thrown file. The sunlight beaming through my office window illuminated the spilled contents. A virtual reality disk had slid out of the file and caught the light. The glint was blinding. How was this missed? Dad didn't store items electronically and would never use a VR disk. I'd been through every inch of that folder over the past few weeks. Where did this disk come from?

Could it be from my doppelgänger? After my suicide, I collided with a parallel world when I crossed over. After I came out of the coma, we stayed connected. Vicky and I call her P-Kate for parallel world Kate. She was instrumental in helping me solve Sarah Alexander's murder. I took out a VR pod from my desk drawer and inserted the disk.

I called out to my condo's virtual assistant. "Tessa, play disc."

The pod whirred, and a video loaded and streamed above my desk. An image of the ground, black Oxford shoes, and then a home came into view a few inches above the pod.

With the shoe shot, it was evident they recorded the crime scene with the lead-tech's body-cam. The house was a projection of the Baxter home, a beautiful mansion from the 1950s.

Affluent was an understatement. The images didn't have the clarity of today's holographic cameras, but still did the job. The tech who had shot the footage continued into the front entry, capturing the vast foyer before entering the den.

The tech walked the perimeter of the room. Every few feet he turned toward the center of the room to document different angles.

An open safe above a white-stone fireplace came into view. He filmed the contents and stepped back to capture the back side of a giant painting attached to the wall. It had an elaborate hinge on one side that ran from the bottom to the top of the frame.

He angled his upper torso down letting the camera capture and record the victim. The body of a Caucasian male lay in a pool of blood. He was hog-tied with a blue silk belt. A naked buttock was visible from a corner of the raised robe. His bald head rested on his right ear. His mouth was open wide in a silent scream. Blue eyes stared back at me. That was the most disturbing part. It felt unnatural to have the eyes open after death. A shudder went through me.

The belt strap and the bottom left edge of the robe were the only indications of its blue color. The rest of the material was blood-soaked, turning it a deep brown. The beige Persian rug beneath him had absorbed most of the blood. It surrounded the upper portion of his frame, like a sloppy chalk outline immortalizing his death. Seeing the image in 3-D versus the photograph I'd been staring at the past few weeks added a depth to the horror in his eyes that made me nauseous.

Fighting to keep the contents of my stomach down, Cooper's low growl didn't register at first. As it deepened, I turned my attention to him and followed his gaze. There was nothing there.

"What's got you spooked, baby?"

Cooper sprang from his bed and stopped short at the entrance to my office. His growl became a snarl. Hackles raised, body low to the ground, he maintained his position to pounce. The hair on his shoulders erect, tiny soldiers standing guard. There was in fact something there. We were not alone.

"Settle, boy, it's okay." Cool air tickled my cheek near my right ear. It was my sign that a spirit was gathering strength to communicate.

I walked around my desk and patted my leg, calling Cooper to me.

"Here, boy, you know the routine. Let's see what our guest wants and send it on its way." Even with the intensity of Cooper's reaction, I hoped it was James.

My pup's obedience training overrode his anxiety, and he sat at my side. His large ears pointed straight up and moved back and forth like antennas. We both jumped as paperwork flew from my desk and swirled around us before settling to the floor. I'd hoped a strong breeze had whipped through the room. A glance at the windows confirmed no such luck. Both were closed.

My psychic skills were developing in baby steps, so seeing ghosts wasn't in my tool kit yet. Sensing them and hearing them was my strength. This felt different. The chill in the room was expected, but there was a thickness in the air that made it hard to breathe. A hot flash kicked in and beads of sweat dripped from my forehead, despite the chill that settled around us.

"Mr. Baxter, is that you? I've been trying for weeks to reach you. Please come through. Why the silent treatment? Why don't you want my help?"

If this was James, he was not only refusing to talk; he was clearly pissed off.

"Say anything. Let me know it's you."

The room remained devoid of sound.

What if he didn't have the stamina to talk, or appear. That could be why he caused the papers to fly!

"James, if it's you, flick the lights on and off, or move something. Give me a sign."

I had instant regret at asking the spirit to move something. I brought my arms up and hugged myself. Partly for warmth and partly because waiting for a ghost to hurl an object across the room gave me the heebie jeebies.

Nothing stirred.

I thought it best to default to what I knew the sprit could move. "If you're not James, please move the papers."

Again, nothing.

Wait, I should have asked James to move the papers. Maybe turning the lights on and off was too much for him.

"James, if it's you, move the papers."

No movement.

The rise in temperature told me the spirit had left. Cooper pressed his bowling ball of a head against my knee with what seemed like all sixty pounds of him, causing me to back away. His eyes stayed fixed in front of us, ears now cowered to the back of his head, affirming what I already knew. There was nothing routine about this visit, this spirit.

No apparition had ever lifted my boy's hackles before. What did Cooper sense that I couldn't? Goosebumps rippled up my arm.

"What have we gotten into, Cooper?"

He licked his nose a few times, to gesture that he was nervous.

I was right there with him. I was getting used to daily requests from spirits to contact loved ones, but it still unsettled me when they first appeared.

He peered at me then around the room. His body relaxed, but only slightly. It was apparent that he agreed with my assessment. Whoever had been here, had left.

The visitor this evening wasn't grandstanding. Anger as heavy as a dense fog pressed down on me like a cement block sitting on my lungs. When the resounding angry vibe came through, it caused me to wonder if we were in imminent danger. The dead could be downright dangerous.

Figuring out what the spirit wanted was priority one. If it was James, why did my desire to channel him upset him? If it wasn't James, then who?

My nerves were on edge. A mug of tea would be a good distraction.

"Tessa, hot chamomile tea."

Tessa responded, "With honey?"

"Yes, just a dab."

Cooper, at my hip, accompanied me to the kitchen. We were both rattled and there was no way he would let me out of his sight. The clink of the ceramic tea cup lowering into the chamber was comforting, as was the light from the setting sun breaking through the bay window. The shifting light softened the honey-yellow walls into a creamy-butter tone.

My mouth watered at the sight of a bag of gingersnap cookies sitting on the center island. A perfect pairing to the steaming cup of tea.

I scooted a barstool closer to the counter and popped a cookie into my mouth, savoring the spicy sweetness before chewing. Next, Cooper received a cookie, and then one more for me, another for Coop until we polished off six of them. Mom always said you could handle everything life threw at you with a bit of ginger and a spot of tea. She was right. The knots in my stomach loosened their grip.

If James came through after all these weeks of trying to channel him, why didn't he want my help? Why wouldn't he want his murder solved? I wondered about his last moments. How long had someone tied him up? Did he lie there in fear, wondering if that was his last night? Did he cling to the remote possibility that his killer would leave him alive? Did he know his killer? The thought of his last moments drained the last trace of energy out of me.

My stomach growled, reminding me it would take more than a few gingersnaps to get through the evening.

"Tessa, dial Vicky."

Within seconds, Vicky's voice boomed from the overhead speakers. "Hello."

"Any chance you could head over with some takeout?"

"On my way," she said.

"You're the best bestie," I said.

"Ditto, see you in a few."

"Tessa, hang up."

Chapter 2

Tessa's voice rang out from an overhead speaker.

"Bffff is here. Shall I welcome her?"

Home units had come a long way with more natural voices, but Tessa still stumbled over slang. Initially, when Vicky's image was programmed into the face recognition software, we associated B.F.F. with the image as a joke. We laughed so hard when the program returned something that sounded like Bffff. I decided to keep it for grins and giggles.

Vicky was more than my best friend forever, she was my mentor. Even though I'd seen Vicky work as a psychic, everything felt different when it happened to me. She made channeling look so natural. Once I got over wanting to hide under the covers, I thought being a medium was the best thing that could happen to a homicide detective. Images of case files closing danced around my head. I didn't expect my body to get hijacked by a rogue spirit, or to have my soul get stuck in another dimension. I would have lost my mind and my body had it not been for Vicky and her psychic development group.

Vicky's holographic image projected a few feet in front of me. She held up two takeout bags from my favorite restaurant, Papa Fu's, for the camera and had an ear-to-ear smile.

"Yes, Tessa invite her in."

"Access granted, please come in," Tessa's voice announced over the door's intercom system.

Cooper heard the click of the lock and beat me to the door. He ran circles around Vicky, anticipating the rawhide treat that always accompanied her visits. The smell of Chinese food permeated the entrance.

"You're a godsend."

Vicky glided past me with the grace of a ballerina. Her long red hair was wild and all over the place, like it hadn't seen a comb in days. It was no surprise that she was wearing a long white skirt and a white blouse with large yellow sunflowers. She always had white and yellow in her outfits. Vicky said white had a spiritual vibration and yellow was warm, sunny, and encouraged growth and creativity.

I followed her toward the kitchen. She stopped short at the entrance to my office, causing me to bump into her. She held up one of the takeout bags and pointed it toward my desk.

"Look at that hot mess. No wonder you haven't eaten. You're right back where you were with Sarah, obsessing over a case at the expense of everything else."

"Uh, giving something my undivided attention is not the same as obsessing. Letting something consume my time isn't the same as letting it consume me. Thank you very much!"

"Don't be so touchy, Katie. I'm right by your side with the Baxter case. You're gonna have to trust me. You've got to pace yourself. Channeling takes a toll. If you keep up the same pace, you're going to crash and burn before your agency gets off the ground. It's a slippery slope between consuming your time and consuming you. The last few weeks, I've watched you pile box after box into your office and plaster the walls with notes and photos, and now the case files are spilling into your home office. It doesn't take a psychic to know you're not sleeping again. You look like crap."

"Thanks. Love you, too." I blew her a kiss.

"You know what I mean. Just admit your obsessing over your father's cold case, just like you did Sarah's."

"Fine. Guilty as charged, can we save the lecture until after we eat?"

I walked into my office and grabbed my electronic tablet.

"Most of the files are scanned." I put my free hand on her shoulder and pushed her toward the kitchen.

Vicky opened the French doors to the kitchen with her elbow and set the bags on the table. Cooper followed, never taking his eyes off the bags.

Vicky scratched him behind the ear. "Too spicy, buddy."

He leaned into her hand to get a deeper scratch. "Who's my favorite Catahoula?" she asked in a sing-song voice, pulling a rawhide treat out of her pocket.

Cooper gave his best sit. She handed him her gift, and he trotted off to his bed. I loved how bonded they were. Vicky gave me Cooper when I came home from the hospital. I had never seen a cattle dog before. "A catawhata?" I had asked when she presented him with pride. She said I needed to have something in my life that needed me. She was a genius. I couldn't imagine my life without sweet Coop.

Vicky pulled chopsticks out of the bag. "These are useless. Pass me a fork, will you?"

I handed her a fork and a plate, and set mine on the island.

"Thanks. How's civilian life treating you?"

It had only been a few months since leaving the department and starting my agency but, in some ways, it felt a dozen years had passed. "Investigating a murder as a PI isn't any different from being a homicide detective. A case is a case. Clues are clues."

"You're just getting started as a third-eye private investigator, you can't stand there and say there is no difference. How many homicide detectives channel the dead?" Vicky air quoted "Third-Eye" for emphasis. It was obvious it still miffed her I didn't call my new agency Third-Eye Investigations.

I had toyed with the name for a while but decided against it. I was still getting used to my psychic abilities and wasn't comfortable shouting to the world that I can talk to the dead. Walk-In Investigations was subtle. It was a play on words. I'm sure the public thought it meant they could step in without an appointment and hire an investigator. Only I appreciated the real meaning; the deceased walked into a medium's body to stream their consciousness and the memories of their death to help solve their murder.

"I'm adjusting okay."

Vicky gave me her not-buying-it look, but didn't press the issue.

"How much sleep are you getting?"

"Still adapting to spirits waking me up all night. Between that and tossing and turning over Dad's old case file, I'm clocking two to three hours a night, max."

"James hasn't come through yet?"

"I'm pretty sure he came through."

She held her hands in the air, in the shape of a "V" for victory. "At last."

"Don't celebrate just yet. He didn't say a word. He just turned my office into a wind-tunnel."

Vicky waved off my doubts. "Your connection to the spirit world is open. That's wonderful."

"You would see that as a positive. Can't say I'd call being haunted a good thing."

"Come on, Katie, stop with the drama. You're not being haunted, you're being contacted. There is a definite distinction. You're a bridge to the other side now. Not the same as a haunting."

"Easy for you to say, you've had this ability your whole life. For a newbie, having spirits around meets the definition of a haunting."

Vicky held up her finger and wagged it at me. "The important fact is you're in communication."

"But on their terms; I have no control. I'm not even sure if it was James. My last case might have been a fluke. What if my brain misfired because of the coma? What if solving the murder as a psychic was a one-off?"

"Patience. Sarah was the first victim you've channeled; it takes time to build the skill. Think of it like building muscles at the gym. You don't get big muscles with one workout. You have to keep at it to see results. Besides, it's not a misfire; it's a permanent re-wire. You said spirits are visiting. That proves you're not a one-time event. He'll come through with details.

You need to relax and keep trying. You'll block messages if you're stressed about it."

"Relaxing isn't my strong point."

"No kidding! You're wound up tighter than that mane of yours. Is your goal to see what you would look like with a facelift?" Vicky tugged at my ponytail.

"Would you stop riding me about my hairstyle?"

"Do I have to remain silent about those shoes as well?" She pointed to my comfortable black loafers.

"At least I don't look like I drove around in a convertible."

She patted at her hair, then shot me the middle finger.

"Bantering aside, taking on a murder Dad couldn't solve may have been too ambitious. Tackling a few recent murders before diving headfirst into a two-decades-old cold case would have been a smarter approach."

Vicky took a bite of food, chewed, and swallowed hard. Her voice softened. "Don't let the fear of disappointing your Dad block you. Age doesn't change a thing. Streaming the dead is streaming the dead. Recently deceased or decades old, it makes no difference. Dead is dead. Doesn't matter when it happened." She nodded to drive her point home.

I took a big bite. My mouth full, I returned her nod; it made sense. The spirit world was not linear.

"Let's take the focus off of James. That may help things shift."

I turned on the tablet and scrolled through the photographs and zoomed in on the traffic-cam image of James on a motorcycle with a female rider. Vicky's attention shifted towards my refrigerator. The tablet's Bluetooth must have been on because the same picture popped up on my refrigerator's electronic display located just above the water dispenser. The refrigerator display synced to my tablet's photos as a screen saver.

Vicky glanced at my tablet and stared at the image for a minute, trying to get a read on it. She looked up at me. "I'm not getting anything. Walk me through the evidence. Let's see if it triggers something. I remember it was your Dad's first cold case as a homicide detective, but I can't remember how the victim died."

"Someone murdered him during a home invasion, or what looked like one."

"If the murderer killed him at home, what's the significance of the traffic-cam shot?" Vicky asked.

"Based on the timestamp, it was the evening of the murder. The medical examiner's report puts the time of death a few hours after. The female may be the murderer or may have witnessed it."

Vicky looked at the photo. "You can't see her face with the helmet visor down, but the small build, purse, and boots are female indicators."

"That, and the forensic analysis found female skin cells on the belt of the robe. They couldn't match the DNA. To make matters worse, there weren't any hits on the fingerprints lifted in the home other than family and staff."

"Any suspects?"

"There were no witnesses who placed anyone with James that night, man or woman. Dad thought James' son Rob had something to do with it but had to drop him as a suspect. He was out of the country in a drug-rehab center, so he had a solid alibi."

"What makes him think it was the son if he was overseas?"

"During the investigation, almost all accounts detailed a strained relationship between the two. Rob stood to inherit half of a multi-billion-dollar estate. His sister, Maxine, told Dad if James hadn't died when he did, it was likely that Rob would have been cut out of the will."

"How could she be sure it wasn't just a threat?"

"They had several fights about his addiction and reckless behavior over the years. A few months before James was killed, he gave his son one last chance to redeem himself.

James sent him to the rehab center he was in on the night of the murder. He paid for it, but with a caveat. If he found out Rob was using again, he was out of the will forever."

"Anything else?"

"There were no other significant leads. Dad said it was an inside job, someone who was close to the family."

"How so?"

"Only family knew about the hidden safe, or that his fingerprint was the only way to open it. Oh, and that brings up a horrid tidbit that the department didn't share with the media; the killer cut a finger off."

"Ouch."

"The autopsy showed it was after the murder, but it's still unsettling."

"What about the sister? She had to know about the safe. Wasn't she in the will? Wasn't she splitting the fortune?"

"Yes, she inherited the other half and was a person of interest. She didn't have the strongest of alibis, but it accounted for most of her evening. When her DNA didn't match the DNA on the belt, Dad turned his attention to finding the mystery rider."

"I agree. My gut is telling me the son knows the rider. We need to figure out her connection."

"Any clues from P-Kate?"

"I think she left a VR disk of the crime scene in Dad's case files or I might have missed it when going through the file."

"Have you tried to connect with P-Kate? She said she would help if you ever needed her again."

"I haven't spoken to her since Sarah's case. She was worried about her world finding out she interfered. I'm hesitant to initiate the contact until I'm certain she left the disk. I don't want to get her in trouble. I was hoping she would reach out to me."

"You don't sound sure it was her."

"It could've been in the folder all along. The CSI tech filmed it. Dad may hate electronics, but everyone else on the team would keep a digital footprint of the case. I'll ask Dad if he recalls seeing it."

Vicky took a bottle of tea out of the take-out bag and inserted a straw. She drew a sip and set the tea on the counter. "She should be able to give signs, symbols, and hints for you to intuit without physical contact, right?

"I would think so. She may be limiting it to dreams. I can't make out what I'm getting. I'm not even sure the dreams are from her."

"What are you getting?"

"I keep having dreams of men's ties and whiskey barrels."

"You're identical to your doppelgänger. What would you assign to those symbols if you were sending them to her?"

"We are not quite identical. She is married to the captain, has a daughter, and is still on the force. I'm very single, no children, and working as a PI."

"Okay, but the way you think is the same. What would you tell her?"

"The fashion today is casual; almost no one wears ties. If I were thinking of ties twenty years ago, you would assign the tie to some occupation."

"And the barrel?" she asked.

"Both the tie and whiskey barrel make me think of wealth. A man of wealth drinking fine whiskey?"

"James was rich," she said.

"Yes, but how is that a hint? It's a fact he was wealthy."

"A tie could be an allegiance," she suggested.

"Like a partnership to kill him? That's what Dad thought."

"You should meet with P-Kate."

"You're right. I'll reach out."

"Have you presented the details to the staff?" Vicky asked.

"Not yet. My stomach knots up thinking about telling them James isn't cooperating. It could shake their confidence in the agency."

She gave me a cold-hard stare. "We merged your agency with mine for a reason. You have a range of psychic talents at your disposal. Why aren't you using them?"

"I know. I would have never solved Sarah's murder without you, P-Kate, or the team."

"You would have. It just would have taken you longer," she laughed.

"Funny woman. I intended on bringing them in when we have James' version to fill in the details."

"You're stalling. You're not a one-person show anymore. Use the team. Everyone is excited and ready to dive in. Let the staff help you figure this out."

"Wouldn't it be better if James filled us in?"

"We can do this without James. Rita can do a remote viewing around the area of the traffic-cam."

"She can get an image from a location in the past?" I was still learning the full extent of each staff member's unique abilities.

"Age isn't a factor. An imprint is forever. I'll consult the tarot cards this afternoon and see if I get any thing," she said.

"Thanks. I'll run this by Dad at dinner tomorrow night and see what he thinks."

"Wow, a meal together. When's the last time you hung out?"

"It's been, at minimum, ten years."

"Are you nervous?"

"No, well ... a little. We were always civil at work, but nothing more than a quick exchange, and he'll be on our team soon. He was impressed with how I solved Sarah's murder and wants to be a part of the agency to help it get off the ground. It's time we got deeper than some comment about the weather we're having."

"Good luck. Tell me what he says. Do you want to be at the office when Rita does the remote viewing?"

"Please. Watching her draw amazes me."

"I'll schedule a meeting in the morning. Do you need Mike there?"

"Yes, let's get everyone caught up. If Rita pulls details of the motorcycle ride, we could use Mike's bounty-hunter skills in tracking her down."

"See you in the a.m. then," she said.

"Sounds good. Give me a ring if you pick up something on the cards that I can share with Dad."

I felt a sense of comfort talking through the case with Vicky. She was right, I was a part of a team now, not a one man show. I was glad she was going to schedule the remote viewing. I smiled down at Cooper as we headed to my bedroom, "See buddy, we're not alone. We have a team."

Chapter 3

I woke up to the smell of coffee. It was a restless night. I had the same dream that I'd had on and off for years, although last night was different. This time I shook myself awake, but only for a few seconds before I would fall right back into the dream. Most nights I lay there paralyzed, despite my efforts to scream myself awake.

Each time I came out of the dream, I tried to stay out. My muscles tensed. I felt like I had clawed my way out of a deep sleep. Hovering between semiconsciousness and sleep, my head was heavy, as though anesthesia coursed through my system, pulling me back in. The moment my eyes closed, the nightmare returned.

It was so real. A hand pinned my shoulder down. An intense pain shot through my right side as the entity shoved his free hand through my lower right abdomen, wiggling his fingers, as if grasping for something specific. His attack was a hard, aggressive tickle, and with a yank, he removed his hand and disappeared. It was never clear what part of me he took, but the pain remained in my side for a few seconds after waking.

My fingers caressed the raised edges of my appendectomy scar until the ache subsided. Was the dream attack a manifestation of my childhood surgery? Did my body shift the invasiveness of the surgery to a dream of being attacked? It took a few deep breaths to return to the present and shift my mood. My breath pulled in a delicious smell, reminding me of the coffee waiting for me in the kitchen.

"Thanks for the espresso, Tessa."

"Good morning, and you're very welcome, Katie."

I nudged my pup. He had me pinned under the covers and wouldn't budge.

"Let's eat, boy."

Cooper stretched before jumping off the bed.

I admit she is a virtual assistant, a floating voice in my condo, but I enjoy our morning ritual.

"Shall I start the shower?" Tessa asked.

"No. Let me get some coffee first. I'm thinking of taking Cooper for a run, and then I'll jump in."

"Very well."

Cooper followed me to the kitchen. I tossed some kibble into his treat-ball and sent it rolling. He ran behind it, pushing it with his nose, stopping to eat the fallen bits. He was a vacuum when it came to food. The toy was the only way to slow him down.

I grabbed the coffee and reached for the creamer option on the exterior of the refrigerator door. *What the?* There was a different picture on display. I went straight to bed without touching the tablet. How did the image change?

"Tessa, what happened to the display on the fridge?"

"You want me to change the display? What would you like to see? The weather? News?"

"No. Not can you, did you?

"No."

I grabbed the tablet from the center island. I turned the unit on. It mirrored the same picture from the refrigerator. It was a crime-scene photo of the Baxter garage. The photo showed two motorcycles parked side by side. I'd taped a copy of the photo to the whiteboard in my office a few weeks ago, but hadn't associated any significance to it. It was just one of the many photos of the Baxter home.

Was it worthy of attention, after all? Who changed the photo on my tablet? Was it James? He didn't seem to want my help. Was P-Kate helping after all?

I selected the folder and air dropped copies of the case file to Vicky, Rita, and Mike. I had a lot to learn about remote viewing but was confident that Rita would be an integral part of the team. I felt lucky both of them were with the agency.

"Tessa, change of plan. Run the water."

"Shower is running, and the towel warmer activated."

"Thanks."

"Anytime."

This clue might help Vicky give me more insights before talking to Dad tonight. He knew the team channeled spirits, but he was a little shaky on how it all worked. One thing was for sure, Dad wasn't ready to know the details about me getting advice from a parallel world.

Cooper ran through his pet door, barking. He must have seen a squirrel. Seeing Cooper running in the yard alleviated my guilt for not taking him for a run.

I took a quick shower, organized the files, and piled everything back into the storage box.

"Tessa, I'm heading to the office. Order a driverless vehicle, please."

"There is one at the Welcome and Leasing Center. It's on the way and will meet you out front. I gave them the address to your office. You're all set."

"Thanks."

"Welcome."

I like to drive, but this morning it was more important to go through the files to analyze the significance of the motorcycles. The picture showed up on the display for a reason.

Chapter 4

I settled into the rear of the vehicle, placed my fingerprint on the pay pad, then opened my tablet. I dragged every image that had a motorcycle into a separate folder and transferred them to a collage template so they could be seen all at once. Of the five photos, why was the picture of two bikes parked in the garage on my display? If any of the photos had a clue to the murder, my money would have been on the photo of James and the mystery rider. Who was she?

I zoomed in on the garage photo. What was the connection? Deep in thought, I hadn't paid attention to the ride. The vehicle made a hard stop as it pulled up to the front entrance. We were already at the office. The door raised. I returned the tablet to the box and stepped out. It was only a few feet to the front entrance, but the weight of the box made the entryway seem much further. When I stepped in front of the motion detector, the glass doors parted granting me entrance. I made my way down the hall to the conference area.

Vicky was prepping for our staff meeting and waved me into the conference room. She took the box from me and set it on the table.

"Grab the tablet out of the box. We have another picture to focus on," I said.

She pulled out the tablet, turned it on, and set it between us. The garage shot was still on the screen.

"P-Kate caused that photograph to show up on my tablet and fridge display."

Vicky studied the photo for a minute, trying to get a read on it. She looked at me. "What makes you think P-Kate caused the photo to show up?"

"James hasn't given me details, so why would he single out a photo?"

"Good point but, until we have confirmation, let's try to figure out this clue. Walk me through your interpretation of the photo's significance. Let's see if it triggers anything."

"Obviously, the picture is from his garage."

"Show me the traffic-cam photo again," she said.

I pulled a hard copy out of the file folder and put it beside the tablet. Vicky would get a better read holding an individual photo versus examining the electronic one.

"Whoa, we missed something last night. Don't you think it's odd she's wearing a helmet and he isn't?" Vicky asked.

"No, it's the law, and the smart thing to do, but not everyone wears them."

"True, not everyone wears them. But if you do wear them, you would have one for your passenger."

We stared at the photo of the bikes parked in the garage. The same helmet the female wore sat on the seat of the bike. In the background, there was a second one hanging on the wall behind the bike.

Vicky broke the silence. "See, two." She tapped each helmet in the photo, causing it to wiggle on the tablet.

"So you think he only had one with him the night of the murder, and he offered her his?"

"Ding, ding, we have a winner. If it were a planned date, they would both be wearing them since he owned two," she said.

"Maybe it was a setup?"

She held the hard copy of the photo. "It could be one of Rob's old girlfriends on the back of that bike, or a school-mate. Someone who 'happened' to bump into James that night. A person his dad would recognize and trust."

"Great observation."

"Thanks. Let's see what Rita picks up." Vicky smiled and set the photo back down. She synced my tablet to the projector's bluetooth and waved Mike and Rita into the conference room.

Rita walked in holding her tablet.

Mike followed at her heels holding his travel mug in one hand and his tablet in the other. He settled on a chair next to mine.

Vicky pointed to the photograph projected on the white screen. "You received this photo in your work folder. It's James Baxter and an unknown female on a motorcycle." She looked at Rita. "It's twenty years old, but we need you to focus on the location and track their evening."

Rita nodded. "Shouldn't be a problem to draw where the ride started or ended."

"Not just the location. Katie is hoping you'll see an image of the rider without the helmet," she said.

"That will be harder. My process returns physical details of a location, but I'll try to pull them in."

Vicky filled them in on the latest updates as Rita stared at the picture. Rita grabbed her stylus and drew the motorcycle and both riders at the traffic light. Man, she was fast. Her sketch had most of the details in the photo. She sketched a series of streets with turn-by-turn directions and ended with a sign for Mount Talbert Park. There was a sketch of a ranch-style house to the left of the sign.

We had a lead! They parked the bike at a neighborhood trail entrance.

"Can you see her face in any of those intersections or at the trail?" I asked.

Rita closed her eyes for a moment and then opened them. "Sorry, no. Just street names."

"Can you send the drawing to my tablet?"

"Done," Rita responded.

"What are you going to do with it?" Mike asked.

"It's a long shot, but maybe the homeowner at the trailhead saw something."

Rita frowned. She was clearly upset that she couldn't provide an image of the female's face.

"Rita, thank you so much. This is a significant clue."

She nodded and gave a slight smile.

"Did you get anything from the tarot cards, Vicky?" I asked.

"No. I even tried to reach James, with no luck. Can you think of any reason he wouldn't want us to solve his case?"

"Nope. Dad said he was a down-to-earth kind of guy. No shady business practices. No enemies to speak of. Nothing to hide."

"Who wouldn't want their murder solved?" Mike asked.

"Well, he could be in a recovery group," Vicky said.

"A what?" Mike asked.

"It's a forgiveness circle. Some souls stay in their group until they decide to continue their karmic ties," Vicky said.

"What do you mean?" Mike asked.

"The group teaches those who have crossed how to best design their next incarnation for their greatest spiritual development. The primary goal is to help spirits forgive past transgressions before they return," Vicky said.

Mike whistled. "That must be one hell of a transgression if it's taking twenty years to forgive."

"Some cuts run deep," I said. I thought of my recent forgiveness of Dad for abandoning me when I needed him the most.

"You know what that means," Vicky said.

"One of us is crossing over to find James," I said.

"You got it."

"Let's leave that as a last resort. Although I'd love to see Mom and my brother Jimmy again, I'm not sure I'm ready to cross back over," I said.

"Totally understand," Vicky said.

"Can we solve this case without James Baxter?" Mike asked.

"Sure hope so," I said.

"What about P-Kate?" Rita asked.

"I'm going to reach out to her since she hasn't contacted me. She was nervous about interfering and may have pulled back. If she can't help, we may have to solve this case the old-fashioned way: feet to the pavement, gum-shoe detective work."

"How did that work for your Dad, the famous Jim Hanson?" Mike asked with a sarcastic tone.

"We have tools he didn't have," I said in his defense.

He shrunk back at the edge in my voice.

I softened my tone. "Let's cross our fingers the homeowner still lives at the trailhead and has security footage from twenty years ago."

Mike shook his head. "Talk about a long shot."

Rita frowned and her shoulders slumped. "I'll keep drawing and see if a face comes through."

"You have given us plenty to go on, don't worry. But... if something does come through, shoot it to my tablet," I said.

Vicky raised her hand. "Mine too."

"Fire it my way as well," Mike said. "I'm sure I'll be tasked with locating her and bringing her in."

"I'll send it to everyone," Rita said.

Chapter 5

I stopped by the house to feed Cooper before heading to Dad's for dinner. He was so happy to see me. I didn't have the heart to set the kibble down and leave again. I waited for him to finish eating, let him out in the yard to relieve himself, and put him in the car with me. He moved back and forth from window to window catching the sights as we made our way to Dad's place. I hoped he wouldn't mind my bringing the pup.

My thoughts turned to dinner. I hadn't had Mom's lasagna, or any lasagna, since she passed. I thought about it all day. Not being much of a cook, even with the recipe, I knew I couldn't do it justice. I didn't want my memory tarnished with some awful version I threw together. I salivated at the mere memory of her homemade tomato sauce. Mom used so much garlic, Dad used to say his throat dried up when he walked into the kitchen. I shook off the memory of Mom in the kitchen and rang the doorbell.

"It's open. Come on in."

I walked in with a six-pack of beer balanced on the box of case files. "Smells delicious," I said.

Cooper ran over to Dad and leaned his head on Dad's leg. He scratched Cooper's ear. "I hope it's okay that I brought him."

"Of course," he moved his hand from Cooper's ear and pointed to the box. "Need a hand?" he asked.

"I've got it," I said. I set the box on the floor and lifted the six-pack.

He wrinkled his nose at the beer. "A nice red wine goes better with lasagna, no?"

I removed two beers and put the rest in the fridge. Not even five minutes in and he is doing it already.

Twelve again, I can't do anything right, can't please him. Only I'm not twelve. I'm an adult. My body straightened, along with my resolve to not let him get to me.

"Consider the ingredients in lasagna, it's a perfect pairing."

He raised an eyebrow, prompting me to continue.

"You have tomato sauce, lots of cheese, garlic, and meat. It's kinda like a nice saucy, sausage pizza. Right? Nothing goes better with pizza than a cold one."

"You could be on to something. Pop a couple of tops. Let's test your theory."

"Yes, sir."

I walked straight to the silverware drawer and pulled out the opener. It was natural to be in the kitchen, like I'd never moved out. Yet a decade had passed since the last time we had dinner together. I opened the two bottles and handed him one. Cooper, resigned to the fact that the scratching was over, laid next to the kitchen table.

"I've been thinking about Mom's lasagna all day. Is it almost done?"

"Ten more minutes and we can dig in. Butter the bread and set the table," he instructed. I cut the French loaf in half and buttered both. I was happy with the busywork to settle my nerves. I didn't want to tell him about my run-in with the spirit. He accepted that I had what he called "unique skills" but was unclear on how it all worked.

"I've been going over the case notes," I said.

"Can you make it work?"

"Yes, with the team's help, no problem."

He didn't comment on the team or ask how they would help.

"What did you think about the virtual-reality disk of the crime scene?"

"It was a typical evidence-gathering recording, nothing that got us anywhere," he said.

Okay, P-Kate didn't leave the disk. It must have been stuck to something, and I missed it until I threw the file. Mystery solved. At least that mystery. Still not sure how the photo changed on the fridge display. "How did his kids,

Maxine and Rob, get along? Seemed like she turned on him, based on her statement," I said.

"Wouldn't say she turned on him. Rob and Maxine's mother died when they were young. The kids were close, well... as close as two opposite people can be. Maxine was a straight-A student, and interested in the family business. She was without a doubt the favorite."

"Was there a wicked stepmother or gold-digging girlfriend in the picture?"

"Never remarried, wasn't one for dating. According to Maxine, James never had a serious relationship after her mom died. She said he didn't advertise it, but her father used an upscale escort service when he didn't want to show up to an event alone."

"What service did he use?"

"It's in the notes. I can't recall the name, but we tested every employee. No match to the female DNA found on the robe tie. Plus, no one from the service had scheduled a date that night. And as you have ascertained from the file, we were never able to identify the female on the back of the motorcycle."

I took the bread and placed it on the table. I wiped my hands on a kitchen towel and lifted the lid off the box, removed the tablet, turned it on and handed it to him. It was still open to the photo of the garage. "Notice the two helmets?" I asked.

"What about them?"

"I'm probably bringing this in from a female perspective, but..." I paused to formulate the best way to broach the new clues. I used the "female perspective" as if to apologize for having thought of something different, something he had not thoroughly investigated.

"Go on," he said.

"I have doubts about the mystery rider being from an escort service or even a planned date."

"Why?"

Not at all sounding defensive, just an innocent question. It was like before Jimmy died, when the three of us played detective. Dad would ask "why" to every idea we tossed at him; keeping us thinking, analyzing, vetting out our thoughts.

"If it were an arranged date, escort or not, wouldn't he have taken her in one of his cars?"

"She could be a biker chick and enjoyed the thrill of a motorcycle." He chuckled.

"She could be. But Vicky noticed in the photos that James owned two motorcycle helmets. If they had planned a motorcycle ride, wouldn't he have had a helmet ready for her?"

"I guess."

"Yet he gives her his, leaving him without one," I said.

He shrugged.

I scrolled through the photos and clicked on the traffic-cam shot. "We know this because the same helmet the rider wore is also in the photo of the bike parked in the garage. In the same garage photo, there's a second helmet hanging from a peg on the back wall." I clicked back on the garage photo and paused for a reaction. None followed.

I continued, spelling out my theory. "If James intended to take her on a ride, he would have used his helmet and given her the second one."

"Good points, but we already established he didn't have a date that night. Credit card receipts showed he had eaten dinner at Rudy's Steak House. Interviews with the staff confirmed he had eaten alone."

"My point exactly." My voice went up a notch and had a deliberate frustrated edge to it. "It couldn't have been a female he was on a date with. He must have run into her after dinner. Maybe someone from the escort service ran into him and took the opportunity to do a little moonlighting."

"Not possible. It wasn't anyone from the escort service. The DNA results on the belt would have come back positive. Remember, we swabbed all employees."

I gave him the same pause.

He took a long pull on his beer. "So what are you postulating here?"

"This was a chance meeting. What if he ran into someone he knew when he was returning home from dinner and they went back to his house? Or since he had a habit of hiring escorts, is it possible he picked someone up on the corner, if you get my drift?"

"A hooker? You think he picked up a hooker? No way, not a chance, not his style."

"How do you know his style? How well do we know anyone? Even those closest to us?"

"Go on," he said.

"Let's say he was into something kinky. A fetish only a stranger would be privy to," I said.

"He would be on his best behavior with the escort service to save his reputation," he said.

"Right. I'm guessing he saved the kinky behavior for girls he hired off the street. His daughter did find him tied up. It's worth looking into," I said.

"You mean it *was* worth looking into."

My brows furrowed at his resistance.

"We can't go back in time to interview and DNA cheek swab every hooker in a fifty-mile radius of his home or restaurant. Those women are long gone. In all likelihood, they're dead by now." His voice deepened. Not quite a defensive tone, but there was a noticeable shift. "We did what we could with what we had."

He held up his hand and one finger at a time, he counted the issues. "One, there was no visual of the female on the back of the bike to present to the restaurant, escort service or media. Two, we had no hits on fingerprints, other than individuals known to have had access to the home. Three, we never identified the DNA on the robe tie. And four, there were no witnesses of James with anyone that night, except for the traffic-cam photo. We had zilch, nada, nothing to work with.

That's unless you count the small build and height, which could have been one of any thousand females on the back of his bike. It was a cold case from the start," he said.

I made a few exaggerated sniffs in the air to break the mounting tension. "Smells like dinner's ready."

He put his beer down hard and opened the oven door.

I leaned on the kitchen counter as he pulled out the lasagna. My mouth salivated. I grabbed his beer and followed him to the table. He placed a more-than-generous helping on my plate, and I didn't object, sitting down across from him and holding my fork in the air, taking a moment to gather my thoughts. If we didn't shift the conversation to something more neutral, this dinner would be a disaster.

"Rob was out of the country but when you first gave me the case file you said you thought he had a hand in it. Is it possible he hired someone?" I asked.

"More in the realm of probable. I'd bet money that Rob hired the girl on the back of that bike, and they were in on it together, somehow. We interviewed everyone he knew, but got nowhere," he said.

"They didn't think Rob was capable?"

"They didn't sing his praises, but they weren't climbing over each other to turn him in either. Think about it. He was about to inherit billions. With that kind of money, there would have been no shortage of people to make a deal with, an old or new friend." He scooted his chair closer to the table. "People have murdered for much less."

"True... So, tell me what's not in the statements. Give me your impressions of the family's reaction to his death."

"He didn't seem to have enemies. Business partners respected him. His staff loved working for him. He was generous and a father figure to some of the younger employees. When he wasn't at work, he was at home. For all his money, he seemed pretty down-to-earth."

Cooper sat up when I reached for a piece of bread. He started drooling and a pool of drool formed at his feet. I tossed him a piece of bread.

"You feed him at the table?"

"It keeps him from drooling," I laughed.

Dad looked at the floor and jumped up and grabbed a kitchen towel. "That drool will ruin my hardwood floor," he said as he soaked up the water. He left the towel at Cooper's feet.

"Lay down, boy," I instructed Cooper. Cooper rested his head on the towel.

"Sorry, Dad. I won't feed him at the table." The edge of Dad's ears were red. I brought his attention back to the case. "And Maxine was the one who found him?"

Dad looked down at Cooper and then back at me. He seemed satisfied the drool fest was over. "Yes. She called 911 but he was already dead."

"When did Rob find out?"

"She called him just before the 911 call."

"Wait, she called him before? Don't you think that's odd?"

Dad shrugged as he chewed his food. "I get why she did it. He was already dead. There was nothing she could do to bring him back. She said she wanted Rob to know ASAP so he could arrange for his flight home. Her next call was 911."

"Where was she that night?" I asked.

He wiped sauce off his chin. "She was at a nightclub, and came home around two-thirty a.m."

"Were you able to corroborate her alibi?"

"We could verify most of it. Maxine was with friends most of the evening but was the last to leave. One of her pals had too much to drink. So, the other one took her home around ten-thirty. The bartender remembered Maxine ordering a martini for last call, which was around one-thirty a.m. Two-thirty a.m. seemed about right, assuming she took time with her drink, and the thirty-minute drive home. It's the missing hours between her friend's departure and last call that we couldn't confirm."

I savored the decadent lasagna and then swallowed. "What's your take on the missing hours?" I asked.

"The opportunity was there, but I don't think she did it. I know people can put on a good act, but what happened devastated her. It wasn't only his death. Her mom's jewelry was in the safe. She was in hysterics when she realized the safe was empty. I'm not sure which one hit her the hardest: losing her dad or losing her mom's jewelry."

"I would hope it was losing her dad over jewelry." I tore off a chunk of bread.

"It's not that she didn't love James. Her mom died when she was young. She said the jewelry held her mom's essence. That it was the only thing she felt connected her to her mom. She had very few memories of her."

"I can relate."

"You have fond memories of your mom. Maxine was so young she barely remembered her."

"I wish we had more time with Mom is all."

"Me too, hon. Me, too." Dad slumped down in his chair. He looked like I had kicked him in the gut.

He sat silently and watched me pull the label off of my beer. I peeled it off in one piece. "Look, one piece. That's good luck," I said.

Dad nodded but didn't say anything.

"Sorry, didn't mean to bring us down. What else was in the safe?"

Dad looked relieved at the shift in the conversation. "A .22 caliber gun and cash. Maxine wasn't sure how much, but said it was significant."

"A .22? That was the same gun that killed James?"

"Yes."

"Why wasn't she a person of interest with the missing hours? It's the same window as the time of death."

"She would have been, but her prints and DNA didn't match those on the belt. Someone else was there that night. Our attention shifted to finding the person on the back of the bike."

"Please tell me you checked Maxine for gun residue."

He shifted in irritation. "Of course we did. No residue."

The edge of his ears turned a bright red again. I had forgotten how he flushed when he was angry. I shifted the conversation to Rob. "What's the story behind the rehab?"

"According to Maxine, James was throwing away money every time he tried to get Rob clean. It wasn't likely Rob could change. He had been in and out of rehab since he was a teen. It wasn't just drug use, though. Rob was a compulsive gambler and had been screwing up since his mom died. He spent his trust fund down to almost nothing."

I took a big bite of lasagna and chewed it slowly, giving me time to process what Dad had shared. "I agree, he had a strong motive. I'm sure Rob knew he couldn't stay clean. No doubt he was a desperate man on the verge of being penniless. Killing James was the only thing that would ensure he'd have funds to support his habits. If you ask me, the cash alone was motive enough," I said.

Dad pointed his beer at me. "That's what my gut tells me, but I couldn't prove it."

"Any big insurance payouts to the kids? Business partners?"

He took a few sips of his beer and shook his head. "Look, I know you have special skills now, this ability to pull a rabbit out of a hat. So, straight up, what did James say? Did you ask him who killed him? We can speculate all day long, but isn't going straight to the source what you do? Isn't that why you left the Homicide Department to start your own Psychic P-Eye agency?" He pointed to his eye when he said P-Eye agency. He didn't know the location of the third eye was in the center of the forehead. We hadn't talked in any detail about the psychic skills acquired after my suicide attempt. I wasn't sure if he was making fun of me or if he was serious.

"I haven't been able to reach him," I stammered.

"What? Are you kidding me? Are you saying you can't talk to the dead now?"

That's all I need, his doubt piled onto mine. Now I had to slay his fears along with my own.

I took a few more bites of lasagna. "I'm relatively new at this, Dad. But don't worry, I'll reach out to the staff on Monday for the best way to connect. I wanted to get your thoughts before I presented it to the team. Anyway, I haven't tried that hard. It's best to gather as many facts as I can before reaching James. I learned on Sarah's case that getting a statement from the dead isn't a slam dunk. Their testimony can be just as flawed as the living's. Sometimes even more blinded because of wanting revenge for their murder. I'm sure with the team's help, we'll reach him soon."

I didn't tell him that James might have come through, but was running silent. My blood pressure spiked at the possibility that it wasn't James. My temples throbbed. If it wasn't James, I would have to cross over to find him. I forced a smile that belied my confidence.

"Makes sense. I'm eager to hear what he says. Let me know, will you?"

"You'll be my first call." Fingers crossed, he bought it.

I shifted the subject. Since Dad was due to join the agency upon his retirement, I needed to get a sense of his confidence now that I had spilled the beans about not reaching James. I hoped his joining the agency would be the bridge that brought us back together, but I also needed his help funding the business. The Department agreed to send me cases but had a limited budget. Dad would handle traditional cases, like catching cheating spouses and corporate probes to help generate funds while I built clients who were open to—less conventional methods.

"Are you still joining the agency when you retire next month?"

"Hanson & Hanson, Crime Fighting Duo. Thirty days until I spy on spouses for a living."

"Dad, don't be flip. Your role is critical in building clients. I'm sure we can get additional homicide departments to send us cases, but we need to expand in the civilian sector. Don't worry. You'll do more than catch cheating spouses as ammunition for divorce cases. Sam agreed to put you down as one of the investigators for the DA's office."

He took a forkful of lasagna and with his mouth full he stammered "Sam? You two back together?"

Cooper looked up at him and then me. He gave a nervous lick. I smiled at him and he placed his head back on the towel.

"Not exactly. We started talking when we worked on Sarah's case. Not to blow your mind, but we even went on a few dates. Nothing that would lead us to getting back together."

"Do you want to get back together?"

"I don't think the option is on the table after I left him standing at the altar."

Dad's face paled. That was the night I had attempted suicide. "Are you okay with that?" he asked.

I took a long swig from my beer. "More than okay. I have no desire to marry Sam."

As far as my unique skills go, I didn't want to expand on that either. He didn't need to know everything in my bag of tricks, or my rabbit hat, as he liked to call it. For now, I didn't see the need to share my ability to look into other dimensions or the fact that my doppelgänger, P-Kate from a parallel world, helped solve Sarah's murder.

Dad held up his hands. "Didn't mean to pry into your love life. Subject closed, and no more shop talk." He took a bite of his garlic bread, wiped dripping butter from his chin, and raised his beer. "You were right. This beer is the perfect pairing with your mother's lasagna. "He winked and pointed his bottle towards me. "Your mom would approve."

A lump caught in my throat. I tapped my bottle against his. "To Mom's lasagna."

Chapter 6

Cooper jumped on the bed and licked my face, letting me know he had been patient long enough. He was more than ready for the weekend. His awareness of time amazed me. I'm not sure how, but I swear that dog can tell time. When it's time for his evening treat, he can tell to the minute when it's eight p.m., and if he hasn't received his evening treat within one minute, he takes his huge paw and punches me in the leg. Then his eyes bore into mine. It doesn't take a telepath to figure out what he is trying to convey. The message couldn't be any clearer: "Excuse me, forgetting something?" And it seems he has the timing of a Swiss watch when it comes to the weekend.

I threw the covers back, slid my feet into my slippers, and looked outside. Minute dust particles danced in a light beam coming in from the patio door. The sun was already high in the sky. Sweet baby Jesus, I slept through the night! I bent forward and touched my slippers, holding the position for a few moments, enjoying the stretch.

Just to let Cooper know how much I appreciated him letting me sleep in, I decided to take him for a run. It would do us both good. Now fully awake, my thoughts raced. The run would help me sort things out. I changed into my running gear, put my hair in a ponytail, grabbed his leash and harness, and we were off toward the town center.

We kept a steady pace. Last night's dinner was the first thought to take center stage. It was a decent first re-connection visit with Dad. Collaborating on the case obscured the fact that we hadn't had a real conversation in a decade.

Could we pick up and rebuild the father-daughter relationship we had before Mom and my brother Jimmy died? It was possible working together could be the bridge we needed. Then again, it could be the match that blew whatever relationship we were trying to revive sky high. It had a fifty-fifty chance of going either way.

Thinking about rekindling our relationship, tension settled into my neck and shoulders. Although the tense moment was short-lived, I was certain it would have escalated had I not steered the conversation to Rob. It was apparent even the slightest shift in the investigation's direction might make Dad feel like I thought he mishandled his original one. I would have to tread lightly.

I thought how I would react and couldn't blame him. Not that he had a fragile ego, anyone would feel second-guessed if someone started picking apart years of hard work.

Not surprising for this time of year, we got caught in the rain twenty minutes into our run. We took refuge at Mike & Darla's Bistro. I couldn't resist the smell of fresh pastries and made my way to an open table beneath the green-and-white awning to wait out the shower.

Darla walked over, holding a water bowl. She lowered it in front of Cooper. "Here you go, sweet angel."

Cooper lapped up the water.

She straightened and took an electronic tablet out of her pocket. "The usual?"

"Yes, one blueberry scone and hazelnut coffee."

"Back in a jiffy."

I zipped my jacket and leaned against the back of the chair, regretting not wearing a heavier coat as the cold from the wrought iron penetrated the jacket and settled deep into my bones. The dark-gray clouds covered the sky. The rain wasn't going to let up for a while. This was definitely a two-cup scenario, maybe three.

I noticed a couple clasping hands at the intersection as they waited for the light to change. The man held his jacket over their heads. *How about that; chivalry isn't dead.* A black Cadillac sped through the intersection as the light turned from yellow to red. The tires sent a puddle of water a few inches above the height of the curb, soaking their shoes. He pushed her back. *Another gallant move. Good man.*

I tried to see the license plate but the driver changed lanes, darted in front of an SUV, and disappeared from view, but not before the traffic camera was activated, sending a burst of three quick red blinking lights. My mind processed what they meant. The cameras were triggered if a vehicle exceeded the speed limit or crossed the center line under a red or yellow light. In a few short days, Mr. Cadillac would receive a fine and two photos: a shot of the front of his vehicle license plate and a close-up of the driver. Smile for the camera, jerk. Smile... for... the... camera!

The picture of James on his motorcycle surfaced in my mind like an antique jack-in-the-box. The case photo of the mystery rider on the back of James' bike had to be the result of a speeding ticket or running a light. How did Dad get a hold of it? Could we backtrack from the intersection and use traffic cameras to figure out where and when the mystery rider's trip began?

I turned to Cooper, my sounding board. "Cooper, biker Chick had the helmet on in the photo, but she wouldn't have had it on when she first climbed on the bike or after she got off and removed it. We had the street names from Rita. We could follow the events of the evening of the murder to a point where she got on before donning the helmet or any point where she got off and removed it or lifted the visor to talk to him at an intersection."

Cooper, ignoring me placed his attention on Darla weaving toward us through the tables. I sat up straight, anticipating the reward headed my way.

"Here you go love."

"Thanks. It smells amazing." I added creamer to the coffee.

"Anything else?" she asked.

"This will do me."

"Holler if you change your mind."

I took a bite, it was just as delicious as it smelled.

"Cooper, do you think I could talk the captain into letting me use the facial recognition software with the DMV feed? We would go back two decades but, if we used James's face, we might glimpse the mystery rider in one of the images. I wanted to see what I could gather from the team before approaching the captain. It was important to provide as many details as possible. Cooper was drooling at my feet. He wasn't interested in the case.

The downpour lifted, but was still too heavy to run in. It would be about twenty minutes before I could get Cooper home without us getting drenched. Nothing to fret over. The scone called my name. One more big bite for me, a small piece for Cooper, and repeat.

Chapter 7

It was weird to knock on the captain's door; it was the first time I had stood here since quitting the force.

"Come in."

I walked in and stood near his desk. "You free, captain?"

He moved his chair around and started to stand like he was going to give me a hug. I stiffened. He froze and sat down. Dang it, opportunity lost. I wanted a hug, but his not being my boss was all new, and I wasn't sure how our relationship was shifting.

"Hi. How ya doing? Miss us already? By the way, it's Nick now. Not Captain." His eyes lit up when he smiled.

"Okay, hi Nick. I'm surprised by how much I miss the department," I admitted. But, I really meant I missed him. I could give a crap about the department. The guys had given me such grief over the years.

"What can I do you for?" He was always twisting his words around. He thought it was funny. I thought it was funny the first few times I heard it.

I picked up a small gun shaped paperweight and made a bang, bang sound, blew pretend smoke away, pretended to holster it, before setting it back on the desk. "Did you get the traffic-cam picture and street names I sent?"

He grabbed the paperweight and placed it closer to him so I couldn't play with it. "Received."

"Any chance you can get footage from the traffic cameras on those streets twenty years ago? It's asking a lot, but I really need to find the female on the back of that bike."

"That's James Baxter in the photo. You started the investigation already? Your Pop is really going to let you do this?"

"Yes."

"Really?"

"It's a long story."

He leaned back in his chair. "Okay, I know long story means 'none ya'."

"It's not that it's none of your business. It's complicated."

"I'm not going to pry," he said.

"Thanks. If you can help me find a photo with her face, we can run it through the facial recognition software," I said.

"I can do you one better."

"Better than the facial recognition program or better than finding a photo with the face?"

"Both," he said.

His right leg was bouncing. Was he excited, or was my presence making him nervous? Was he trying to figure out our relationship as well? Things had shifted since I learned P-Kate had married the captain in her world. *Focus, Katie. In this world, you and the captain are just friends.*

"I'm intrigued. What have you got for me?" I said.

"What does your afternoon look like?"

"For you, it's wide open."

"My college roommate is an IT tech and has a pilot program that I think will help."

You've got to keep what you see a secret. Can you promise that?"

"Scouts' honor." I held up three fingers.

"Come with me." He grabbed his gun, phone, and coat.

"Where are we headed?"

"I'll tell you when we get there."

"Are you going to blindfold me?" I giggled like a schoolgirl.

"Maybe." He laughed.

We walked out of the building, and a cold wind sent chills through me. I buttoned my jacket. Nick drove a red pickup truck. He opened the passenger door and waved me in. I had to grab the handle and hoist myself in.

"Buckle up, missy."

He was in an unusual jovial mood.

We drove about 50 minutes out of town. He pulled into a curved driveway. The home was a one story, modest house with a sitting area on the front patio.

"One-story home in a subdivision? That doesn't seem top secret. No mystery basement thirty levels down?"

"Better to hide in the open," he said.

"Now you've really got my curiosity piqued."

Nick rang the doorbell. A stylish woman in her thirties greeted us, or rather the captain. She barely glanced at me. She batted her eyelashes. "Good afternoon, Nicholas. Paul is expecting you." She kissed each cheek. Her voice purred his name.

Nicholas? I had never heard anyone call him that. It was usually captain or Nick. And that sex-kitten voice. Were they dating? Was that jealousy I was feeling?

"Jenny, this is Katie. Katie, this is Paul's kid sister."

She gave a curt nod in my direction. "Afternoon." Her voice, now lacking in purr, had a dismissive tone.

"Afternoon." I nodded back.

Jenny punched his arm. "Come on now, I'm not a kid anymore. She glanced down at her cleavage. You haven't been away that long," she gave a flirty laugh.

I could tell Nick was making every effort not to follow her gaze to her breast. "Um, where's Paul?

She frowned and seemed disappointed that he didn't play along. "In the basement. You know the way."

Nick put his hand on the small of my back and guided me to the kitchen and opened a closed door. Halfway down the stairs I could see why I needed to keep a secret. I felt like I stumbled into a high-tech war room. At least 20 large monitors had various live feed surveillance videos going.

"Thanks. Your girlfriend seems sweet, Nick-o'-las." I couldn't resist drawing out the name.

"She's not my girlfriend." He smiled and seemed to enjoy my noticing she used his full name.

Paul met us at the bottom of the stairs. He was the opposite of Nick. He was a large burly man with a long, bushy, woodsman-like beard. Without any strain or effort, he lifted Nick a few inches off the ground and gave him a bear-hug and dropped him back down. Then they did some kind of fist-bump-hand-motion thing. Nick adjusted his coat after the manhandling, not at all flustered by the exchange.

"That's some secret handshake you have there," I stifled a smile.

"Does she know she can't tell anyone what she is about to see?"

"She… has a name, Katie," I said, reaching out my hand to shake his, stepping back just enough to keep him from lifting me.

"I'm going to need the secret handshake," he said, holding out his fist, waiting for a bump. "Don't leave me hanging, Ms. Katie."

I gave him a fist bump and tried to remember the shaking finger-hand part. "What are you guys, a couple of ten-year-olds?"

"Eleven, but who's counting?" Paul walked to his desk and sank into a large, leather, overstuffed office chair that would have dwarfed most people. With his size, though, it was a natural fit. "Let's see that photo."

Nick handed him the photo of James and the mystery rider. "Here you go. Make me proud."

Paul scanned the photo onto his desktop and cracked his knuckles. "Ready for the magic?"

We gathered around his monitor. He took the photo from his desktop and transferred it to a folder labeled ORDB. A program opened, and a grid overlaid the photo. Paul clicked on a box around James' face, the helmet, the mystery rider's boots, and her purse, and clicked "send." Within minutes, the reason for his behavior became clear. There were fifty or so photos rotating across the screen. The same woman's face appeared in multiple photos. Even photos with the two of them on the bike in the background of strangers' selfies.

Nick held his hand up for a high-five. "You da man."

Paul high-fived and said "Mad skills to the rescue."

I hadn't seen this side of Nick before. He was always so formal and serious. The reason for the exchange sunk in, and I hit Paul's shoulder. "You have a hit?" My voice was high-pitched like a twelve-year-old boy that had just hit puberty. I deepened my voice. "How? Who is she?"

"The 'how' is a software program I built based on facial recognition software. I added object recognition a few years back, and it increased the number of hits exponentially." His smile was ear to ear. I wasn't sure how he was able to keep this a secret. He did a happy dance. "This software is going to make me rich."

I was dumbfounded. "Object recognition? How are you doing this? This photo is twenty years old, and these results aren't from traffic cams." I pointed to a photo on the screen. "That's a person's selfie, and James and this woman are showing up in the background. How is that possible?"

"That's the beauty of the program. The photos are from federal buildings, banks, schools, any business with a camera, and any photo uploaded to the cloud or sent via text, air drop, or email. Any photo with a combination of her helmet, boots and purse and James' face is pulled into the program and sorted by date and location. This is the part you can't tell anyone, or we'll have a riot on our hands."

"You're not lying. Big Brother is watching." Nick said.

"It's a sign of the times. After the bombings of 2030, Homeland Security developed software that crawls the web and pulls back any photo uploaded from any source, or stored on any server. Even little Johnny's fifth birthday party at the local pizza shop in small town USA. Every photo is classified as in the 'interest of National Security' with no destruction date for future scrutiny, should the need arise. With a bit of hacking, my program has a direct link to that database. A few filters, a simple query, and I can pull back every photo in that database that meets my criteria."

"Every photo?" I gasped.

"Affirmative." Nick slapped his desk a few times and spun around in his chair. "Now watch. Thanks to my software, we have her face. I'll add it to the facial recognition filter and narrow the search to the date of the murder." About half of the photos rotated off the screen. Twenty photos remained to include a driver's license photo. He clicked on it. "There's your mystery woman."

I read the driver's license. "Sabrina Mitchelle. This is unbelievable."

"That it is," Nick said.

"These photos are all from the night of the murder? Can we sort them to see if we can build a timeline?"

He moved pictures around.

"Enlarge that one." I pointed to Sabrina and James pulling out of a garage on the back of his bike. "And that one." I pointed to her pulling out of the garage in a red compact car. "Can you zoom in on her face?"

He clicked on her face, enlarging it three or four times.

"Man, she looks terrified. Do you agree, or is it just me?"

They both nodded.

"What is the timestamp on each of those photos?" I asked.

"She left the garage on his bike at 5:06 p.m." He pointed to a third photo. "You can see from this photo she's entering the garage on foot at 11:49 p.m., close to midnight, and then exited in her car a few minutes later."

"She entered on foot?"

He selected a fourth photo and fifth photo. He rubbed his beard. "These might explain it. There is footage from James' security camera. It shows her arriving at his house on his bike and leaving 25 minutes later on foot."

"Are you sure that's her? You can't make out the face. It's too dark."

"See the boots and purse in the photo? Same height, same boots, and purse. Object recognition."

"Are you sure it's his camera? Why wasn't that in the police file?"

"Am I sure? You doubt me, Ms. Katie?"

"No. I..."

"I'm just messing with you. It's his. The photo is stamped from the IP address of his security camera. Since you can't see her face, maybe they didn't see value in adding it to the file."

"You can tag an IP address from a photo?" I asked.

"If it was loaded on a server or available to view through a website, I can."

"Really?"

"Yep," he said.

"Where is the garage?" Nick asked.

Paul zoomed in on an image. "Happy Valley Outlet Mall,"

"How far is that from his house?" I interjected.

Nick clicked on a travel icon. "About five miles."

I pointed to a photo showing the boots. "Look at the heel on her boot. She walked five miles in those?"

"Guess so," Nick said.

I could tell they had no idea of the significance of walking five miles in heels.

"Is the address on that license where she lives now?" I asked.

He opened another program and entered Sabrina Mitchelle. She had several name changes, not uncommon with multiple marriages. Sabrina Mitchelle, Sabrina Daniels, and Sabrina Foster were associated with her file. He clicked on Sabrina Foster. A copy of her active Oregon driver's license came into view, along with her employment history and family history. Her birth certificate showed Sabrina Mitchelle. A marriage license showed Sabrina Daniels, married to Victor Daniels. An application for a name change showed she returned her name back to Mitchelle a few years after her first marriage. A second marriage license showed her as Sabrina Foster.

"Is Victor dead? She's married again, but no divorce papers."

"Good catch. No, Victor still lives in Seattle."

"She moved several times over the years, but is still in Portland. She's married with two children and works as a paralegal for an insurance-defense law firm. She had no arrests for prostitution," he said.

Nick added, "She could be the girl next door."

"Agreed, she was in her second year of community college at the time of the murder and held down several waitressing jobs since she was sixteen," Paul said.

He printed the documents, placed them into an envelope, and made another set for Nick.

"Remember, you can't share how you got this information with anyone." He looked at me and then at Nick. "Either of you."

"It will go with me to the grave. I swear," I said.

He handed me the envelope.

Nick grabbed his copy. "Lips are sealed."

"Yes, I understand. Thank you so much, Paul. I'm so grateful to you. More than slightly horrified at the same time, but grateful." I tucked the envelope in my purse.

"I hate to ask for more, but we need to know what happened on the way to his house and more about her walk back to the garage. You're going to have to convince me she walked five miles in heels. Plus, I want to establish a turn-by-turn timeline before I contact her. If her story deviates in any way, I'll know she's lying. Can you trace where they were for six hours?" I asked.

"It can be done, but compiling a structured timeline takes a lot longer," he said.

"It's possible they went to Mount Talbert," I said.

They gave me a blank stare.

"It was one of his favorite spots, based on the case notes," I offered, not wanting to explain Rita's remote viewing exercise.

"That may reduce the time, but it will still take most of the night," Paul said.

"I can wait," I said.
"Me too," Nick said.
"Settle in. I'll order us some pizza."

Chapter 8

I was groggy from overeating and closed my eyes for a few moments.

Paul nudged my shoulder, waking me from a deep sleep. I was out longer than I thought and wiped my eyes.

"I have as much of the timeline as I'll get."

Nick must have dozed off as well because he jerked upright at the sound of his voice.

"Welcome back, sleeping beauty," Paul said.

"What do you have?" I asked.

"I composed more details from the photos, and you nailed it. They were at Mount Talbert." He recounted the streets they took and estimated how long they were at each location. "Looks like the trailhead is in James' neighborhood. I got an image from a home security camera near the entry, and you were right. They parked there that night."

Rita was dead-on with her drawing, shoring up my confidence in her and the agency.

"I wondered how they knew each other. She makes less then 80K a year now and was living off of student loans and pulling in less then 25K at the time of the murder. I checked out her current neighborhood with a satellite street view. It's modest. She doesn't seem like she had the means to hang with James' circle. I ran her finances to see if she came from money. She comes from a middle-class background. She has a stable work history and has been with the same insurance law firm the past five years. I can't figure out what the two had in common that he would ride her around or take her home," Paul said.

"So, there was nothing in the file to show that she received a payoff or that she knew any of the relatives before that evening?" I asked.

"No, I couldn't find any photos or paper trail showing contact with any kin, before or after the murder."

"A one-night stand that went wrong?" I said.

"That would be my guess," he said.

"I wish I could repay you."

He looked at me and then winked at the captain. "Actually, you cleared a debt."

Nick nodded to Paul in agreement.

"How did I...?"

Paul interrupted me. "Never you mind. I hope it gives you what you need to solve the case."

"I can't see how all of this data won't."

"Alrighty, you two get out of here. I've got to get some sleep."

I gathered my things and slid my purse strap over my shoulder. "Then I guess it's goodnight."

Paul walked us to the front door and shook Nick's hand with a massive pump. "We good?"

"We're good," he said.

It seemed formal compared to the earlier bear-hug.

I gave Paul a hug or a partial one. I couldn't wrap my arms around his girth.

Nick opened the truck door for me.

I grabbed the handle bar and started to hoist myself into the seat. I stopped. "I owe you. How long have you known about this incredible software?"

"For a year or so, but it's the first time I have asked for access to it."

"Wow, why now?"

Nick gave the front tire a small kick. "Ethically, until he sells the software to government agencies, and links to databases without hacking, I can't use him for the department's cases. I figured since you're no longer under the department, we could use your case as one of his pilots. He owed me a favor, so I cashed it in."

"I wondered what the debt talk was about. You cashed in your chip to help me?"

"That I did."

"Why?"

"You gonna look a gift horse in the mouth, Hanson? Why does it matter?" He softened his tone. "It seemed important to you, to your dad, to your relationship with him."

"It is. Thank you so much."

"You're welcome. I just wish my dad were alive, so I could try to mend our old wounds. You should reconcile with him if you can. I can't tell you the regrets you'll have if you let that opportunity pass."

"I know. You're not the first person who has told me that."

"If you hear something more than once, then it's a message you should heed."

"I'll keep that in mind, Yoda," I said, trying to lighten the mood.

"There is no try, do or do not," he said in his best Yoda voice.

"You're a *Star Wars* fan?"

"It's a classic, good versus evil. He laughed. How could I not be?"

"So true."

"Speaking of good versus evil, what's your take on her? Are you gonna bring Sabrina in?" I asked.

"That's my intention."

"I know she works for an insurance defense firm and not a criminal law firm, but I'm concerned she's going to lawyer up and we'll never find out what happened that night," I said.

"So, what are you proposing?"

"I think she'll be more open if I stop by as a private investigator gathering details on a cold case versus you hauling her in and putting her under the spotlight."

"You know we don't use spotlights."

"Figuratively," I said.

"Be careful and bring a gun. Sabrina may look like the girl next door, but don't relax your guard. I want a full report as soon as the interview is over. Do you want me to have an unmarked car outside during the interview?"

"What? No, I can handle this. I'll bring my gun. Thanks again for helping me find her."

He winked at me. "You're welcome. Now let's get you back to your car."

I got in the passenger seat and looked up as he leaned in. For a moment, I thought he would kiss me, but he just shut the door and made his way to the driver's side. I was surprised that I was disappointed.

Chapter 9

The next morning, I busied myself organizing the case file with the new documents Paul provided. Reviewing the file would help me give Dad a good picture of the timeline and also pass time until I interviewed Sabrina. I didn't want to approach her at work and figured the best contact would be a cold call at home. When I couldn't stand it any longer, I drove to Sabrina's house, parked the car a few houses down, and waited for her to return home. I hoped the element of surprise would be in my favor.

Sitting in the car for a few hours, memories of past surveillances flooded to the surface like a tsunami. I thought about the many partners I had over my career. After a few months, most requested a new partner. A few lasted a year. It's not that I was a problematic partner. I just enjoyed working alone. My colleague Walter summed it up in a nutshell. The way he put it, "my dogged determination and lack of personal life" were too intense for most.

The comment wasn't fair. I had a personal life and was even engaged. The difference was I didn't sit around complaining about my relationship, so they assumed I didn't have one. I didn't need to complain. Sam's career was just as important to him as mine was to me. He understood that murders don't occur Monday through Friday, leaving the weekends and evenings free for family obligations. They shouldn't resent me because they married spouses or had mates who couldn't understand or appreciate the job wasn't a nine-to-five career.

I looked at the case file on the passenger seat. The edge of a photo peeked out from the side of the file. I pulled it out. It was Sabrina exiting the garage. My gut told me this was not the face of someone who had just killed. Her eyes were filled with terror. She may not have murdered him, but she saw something that made her take off on foot and walk five miles to her car.

Sabrina drove past me in a blue SUV. I waited until her garage door opened and closed again before exiting my vehicle. I rang the doorbell. The door opened and she stood in the gap of the door and frame. Before I could say who I was, she pointed to the no solicitation sign. "What is it with you people? Is that too big of a word for you? It means...."

I held up my hand to stop her tirade. "Sabrina Foster?"

"Yes?"

"My name is Katie Hanson. I'm a private investigator." I handed her my card. "I would like to talk to you about James Baxter."

She didn't take the card. Her face went pale, and she grabbed the door frame.

"Are you all right?" I slipped the card in my pocket, stepped toward her, and held my arm out to catch her if she fainted.

She let go of the door frame and regained her composure. "Who?"

"James Baxter was murdered twenty years ago. The department reopened his case."

"I'm sorry, I don't know anyone by that name. I can't help you. I don't mean to be rude, but I have to start dinner," she said as she tried to close the door.

I put my foot in the crack and handed her a picture of the two of them. "Does this photo refresh your memory?"

She didn't answer.

I pulled another from my pocket. "How about this one?" I handed her the picture of her leaving the garage.

She stared at it but didn't respond.

"Trust me when I say I am the one you want to talk to. This is a courtesy call. I don't think you had anything to do with his murder, but the Homicide Division doesn't share my sentiments. If I can't provide something compelling and concrete, they may decide to charge you for his murder. Now is there somewhere we can talk?"

"My daughter is at cheer practice, and my husband won't be here for another hour. Promise to leave before they come home?" She opened the door to me.

"You have my word."

I followed her through the living area into the kitchen. The house was simple but tastefully decorated. A large canvas painting of Sabrina, her husband, her son, and daughter hung over the fireplace.

I pointed to the canvas. "Beautiful family you have."

"Thanks." Her voice cracked. "They're my world. I'll tell you what I remember, but I don't want my family to know what happened."

I was right; all these years later, the terror in her voice reinforced what I saw in her eyes.

She opened the freezer and extracted a large bottle of vodka. Her hands trembled, causing the bottle to tap the edge of the glass a few times as the liquid rose well past the center. She set the container down and added just enough orange juice to change the color. "I don't usually drink this early." She held up a second glass. "May I pour you one?"

"No, thanks." *Was that a true statement or did she have a habit of drinking doctored 'OJ' in front of the children?*

"Sit," she motioned to a chair next to a small kitchen table.

I took out my phone to record our conversation.

"I'm sorry. I won't consent to a recording."

"No problem." I put it back, pulled out my tablet, and sat across from her. I tapped the menu and selected the virtual keyboard function. An image of a keyboard projected from the bottom of the unit. I placed my hands over the projection.

"Start from the beginning. How long did you know Mr. Baxter?"

"I met him the night of the photo you showed me. I didn't kill him. I swear. He was alive when I left. I checked his pulse."

"Why did you check for a pulse if you didn't shoot him?"

"Shoot him? I hit him over the head with a vase."

I stopped typing.

"Then how did he die of a gunshot wound?"

"How would I know?"

I put my hands back over the keyboard. "Let's start at the beginning of the evening. How did you meet?"

I chose not to acknowledge her comment that she didn't commit the murder. I did make a note that she provided details explaining the broken vase found near his body.

"I spent a few hours walking in the outlet mall. When I got out, I lost my bearings and couldn't find my car. After walking four levels, panic set in, and I burst into tears. Mr. Baxter drove by on his motorcycle and stopped because he saw me crying. He offered to drive me around the garage so I could hit the car remote, and we would follow the sound to my car. I told him I had tried that, but the sound was echoing, and I couldn't pinpoint the sound. He said we would drive by every car on each level until we recovered it. I was scared at first, but he had the kindest, saddest eyes. He reminded me of my best friend's father, and my feet were killing me, so I agreed. It took a while, but we found my car."

"Then what happened? How did the rest of the evening go?"

"We talked for a few minutes by the car. I shared that I was new to Portland, and he offered to show me a spot nearby that had a beautiful sunset. I hesitated, but he told me it was his wife's favorite, and he missed her so much. He hated going there alone. It just reminded him of how lonely he was. It was a stupid thing to do. He could have been a serial killer, but I trusted him. His downcast eyes were heavy with sorrow. You can't fake the eyes. They were a reflection of his soul. Do you know what I mean?"

I nodded.

"So, I got back on his bike."

"You went to Mount Talbert?" I looked up from typing.

She seemed startled that I had uncovered that fact. She downed half of her drink.

"Uh, yeah, the view was from Mount Talbert. We stayed there until sunset. I shared that I moved to Portland from Seattle after an abusive relationship and opened up about the horrible things my ex did to me. He talked about his deceased wife and their fairytale life and romance. He seemed upset about what I had endured and said he prayed that I would find someone as loving as his soulmate. I can't remember her name. His show of emotions and his undying love for her tugged at my heart. I had a moment of hope that there were a few good men left in the world. Sad to say, my hopes were dashed."

"Go on."

"After sunset, I thought we would head back to the garage. We got on his bike, and he told me he wanted to take a quick detour. He said that he lived in the neighborhood and suggested a glass of wine before taking me to my car. Again, I know it was stupid, but after spending a few hours with him, it just felt safe. I was lonely, and we seemed to hit it off as friends despite the vast age difference."

I looked over at the coffee carafe on the counter. "Is that fresh? Can I get a cup of that?"

She followed my gaze. "My daughter makes a pot before her cheer practice. Usually, around 3:30 before she heads out. It gives her energy. Where are my manners? Creamer?"

"Please."

She filled a mug with coffee and selected milk from the refrigerator dispenser.

"That's enough," I called out.

She carried the mug over. "Here you go."

Out of habit, I blew on the coffee before taking a sip. "Thanks. What happened when you got to the house?"

"He gave me a tour of his wine cellar. We stayed down there for a few minutes, and he tried to educate me on the different wines. He wiped the dust off a bottle and told me he was opening his finest vintage as a celebration of my new life in Portland. My tastes were at the level of boxed wine, so I took his word for it."

"What happened next?"

"We each had two glasses of wine. James excused himself and said he had to take a nature break. When he came back wearing a robe, I freaked out and asked why he had changed. I demanded that he bring me to the garage. He refused, stating it was late and the alcohol made him tired. He told me to spend the night in the guest room. He promised to take me first thing in the morning. I told him I didn't want to stay. I begged him to take me home."

"Did he take you home?"

"No, he apologized and confessed he misread our connection. James said he was a foolish old man for thinking I would be interested in him and told me not to worry. He had no intention of hurting me."

I locked eyes with her in concern. "Did he hurt you?"

"He didn't. He had too much to drink and didn't think it was safe to drive. He promised to take me back in the morning. He insisted I wear a pair of his daughter's pajamas and stop whining about leaving."

"Did you stay the night?" I wanted to see if her story matched the timeline we uncovered.

"No. I told him I would call for a ride. He got angry and told me not to be foolish. I tried to run past him to the front door. He grabbed my arm and asked me to listen to reason that he would take me back in the morning. His grip was so tight. I thought he would never let go."

"How did you escape?"

"A vase from an end table was right next to me. I hit him over the head with it. He fell on his knees before collapsing. He was unconscious, but breathing. I was afraid he would wake and chase me, so I tied him up with the belt from his robe. I washed my glass and put it in the dishwasher and wiped my prints from anything I touched."

"How did you get to your car?"

"I walked, following a navigation app."

"Why not hail a ride share?"

"I thought he would find me. I never gave him my last name. He was a rich man, and that comes with power. I didn't want him contacting cabs or ride shares around his area and paying them for my address for revenge or who knows what. He was acting crazy. James was alive when I left."

"Did you know someone murdered him that same night?"

"How could I not? It was all over the news. I couldn't come forward. I swear on my mother's grave that I didn't shoot him. I've never even owned a gun. You see why I couldn't go to the police, right? Who would ever believe that I knocked him out, tied him up, and someone else came along and shot him? It's ludicrous. No one, absolutely no one, would buy that."

"It seems farfetched, I'll admit. Let's go back to your ex. You mentioned you moved to Portland because of an abusive relationship. Did you ever press charges or file a report?"

"Yes, I have two reports on Victor. A neighbor called the police, but I didn't press charges. It was our first intense fight, and he had me convinced that I'd triggered him. He had this way of twisting everything so that before the argument was over, I was apologizing for making him crazy."

"I never thought I would be that person who wouldn't walk away at any sign of abuse. He was good at manipulating. It was a gradual transition. Each time was subtle. It took me longer than it should've to catch on. It started with my friends were annoying, and we needed to find new couples to hang with. Over time, everyone stopped calling when I kept declining invites. Then my family became the target. They were too intrusive into our lives; didn't I want to grow up and be independent? He said things like *shouldn't someone my age drop the daddy's girl routine?* Once he had me isolated from my friends and family, the violence started. In the beginning, he would just push me or make a motion with his fist like he wanted to punch me. Then he stopped making the motion and hit me for real."

"How long did that go on?"

"Longer than it should've. However, the second time the police came out, Victor told them I had too much to drink and was throwing things at him. He pointed to the bruise on my wrists and said he had to hold my hands down trying to calm me. It's true. I was more than tipsy, but I didn't throw anything."

"I can't imagine how trapped you felt. Why did he say that?"

She drew two big pulls of her booze. "We were having a nice dinner. Everything was perfect until we left. When the attendant opened the car door for me, I climbed in thanking him. As soon as we turned the corner, Victor slapped me on the side of my head. He said I intentionally flirted with the valet, by letting my skirt ride up when I got in the vehicle, giving him a thrill. I should have known not to react, but I didn't think. Before I could stop myself, I shouted *try getting in this small car with a skirt and see how high it hikes up.'* I never raised my voice to him before. That triggered him. He punched me a couple of times and at one point he slammed my head against the passenger window.

When we got home, he dragged me by my hair, into the house, throwing me on the floor. I laid crying, too afraid to move. Victor left me for a few moments to fix a drink. He came back for me, pulled me to the family room, shoving me into a chair. He handed me a whiskey glass and ordered me to down it. I told him I didn't want it. He kept pushing it in my face, and I knocked it out of his hand, shattering the glass."

Sabrina walked over to the counter and snagged a tray of cookies, removing the cover and placed them in front of me.

I reached for a cookie and held it up. "Thanks." I sipped my coffee before I took a bite. "And that's what he meant when he said you were throwing things?"

"Yes, that was his version. He snatched me by the hair again, locking me in the bedroom to 'settle down.' It wasn't like me to be so fearless and call 9-1-1. I'm sure he looked bewildered when he answered the door, but being a psychopath, he recovered without missing a beat. He let the officers in and unlocked the bedroom to show them I was all right. He told them he bolted the door for his protection while motioning to the shattered glass."

"There is a lock on the bedroom door? Did he lock you in often?"

"We had locks on every door in the house because his son used to steal from him."

"Did the officers buy his story?"

"One asked if I had broken the glass. I nodded, but before I could explain, Victor said to the cops, 'There you have it. She just admitted it.' Then he shut the door on me. This time he didn't lock it. I waited a minute before I came out. I wanted to call them back, but he gave me such an expression of contempt I froze. He spoke through clenched teeth and instructed me to say goodnight to the gentlemen and to apologize for wasting their time. I did as he said. His voice frightened me." Her hands shook.

"He walked them out. I overheard him say I'd be fine in the morning after I slept it off. He chuckled and added, 'I'm sure you've seen a female or two go bat shit crazy with a few drinks in them.' They laughed with him."

"What happened after they took off?"

"He was furious. He strangled me until I blacked out. When I woke up, he was spread out on the couch staring at the TV. I waited for him to fall asleep, grabbed my purse, keys, and ran. My parents took me in. He continued coming by their house and my work. I had a domestic violence protection order against him, but it didn't stop him. He just stayed a few feet beyond the limits. My parents were elderly, the strain and worry for my safety gave my dad a heart attack. He recovered, but I couldn't put his health at risk again."

"Is that when you moved to Portland?" I polished off the cookie.

"Yes, it was the best option. I wanted to be as close to my parents as possible if they needed me."

"I know it must have been hard to leave your parents and your life in Seattle. You did the wise thing. The statistics of ex-boyfriends or spouses murdering their wives or girlfriends would shock you."

"I know the statistics. It's why I left. Getting a place by them in Seattle was ideal but everyone kept telling me not to ignore the danger I was in—my family was in."

"Did you divorce him?"

"No, I changed my name back to my maiden name but never divorced him. He would never have agreed to one. I just wanted to disappear."

"Look, I know this sounds like something straight out of a stalker movie, but is it possible he followed you to the Baxter home? He may have assumed the two of you were dating and, after you left, went in to rough up your date to scare him off. When he found him tied up, he took advantage of the opportunity and shot him. It doesn't just happen in the movies."

"I had no indication that he knew I was in Portland. I never saw him, and he didn't have my new phone number. Once I moved from Seattle, he never contacted me. I'll admit that he is more than capable of murder, but I can't be positive it was him."

"I wouldn't be too hasty to discount him. Moving a few hours away isn't enough of a deterrent. Stalkers move across the country, pursuing their targets. A handful of hours is a short drive," I said.

"What happens now? How do I keep my family out of this?" Her voice quivered, and tears welled.

"If you did nothing wrong, what do you have to hide?"

Tears threatened to spill over. "You know the media. It doesn't matter if I'm innocent. They'll camp out at my door and follow us everywhere, shattering our lives. My husband knows about Victor, but the kids don't. If this gets out, Victor will find me."

Not to mention bigamy charges, I thought. I handed Sabrina a napkin from the holder on the table. She dabbed at her eyes, soaking up the tears.

"I don't have control over the media. I'll see what I can do to keep this from going public. As for what happens next, you have to come to the station."

"Why?"

"They'll want a formal statement."

"Can't you just tell them what I said?"

"It doesn't work that way. They need to record it and, even though you admitted to being there and using the robe tie, they will ask you for your DNA and fingerprints."

"Are they going to put me in jail?"

"I doubt it. If the department was adamant about arresting you, they wouldn't have let me come here first. This shows the detective is open to getting the facts and making a decision."

I didn't mention we wanted to get as many details as we could before she clammed up at the advice of her attorney. Her account didn't deviate from the timeline Paul compiled. That was in her favor. Had she made any revision; it would be impossible to convince Nick that she was innocent. I trusted her and hoped her statement and DNA would be the end of it. Anything deeper, and we wouldn't be able to keep the media out of it.

Chapter 10

I swung by Dad's to share the good news. We were no closer to identifying the killer, but we knew who the mystery rider was and that she didn't kill James. I gave Dad a heads up that I was on my way. He left the door cracked open a few inches.

I poked my head in. "Dad?" No answer. I stepped in.

"Dad? You home? Sorry I took so long to get here. I wanted to feed Cooper first. Dad?" I closed the door behind me. "Daaaaadddd?"

A loud noise reverberated from the kitchen.

I ran in, praying I wouldn't find him on the floor with a broken hip or, worse, clutching his chest. I found him under the kitchen sink, hitting a pipe with a wrench.

"Dad, for Pete's sake. Why didn't you answer? You gave me a heart attack!"

"What? Why?"

"You're not getting any younger, and I expected you fell or worse." I grabbed the flashlight from the counter and aimed it at the pipe he banged on. "What are you doing, anyhow?"

"What the hell does it look like I'm doing?"

"It looks like you're about to bust a pipe and flood your kitchen."

"I know what I'm doing. And thanks for assuming the worst. I may not be a spring chicken, but I'm not a frail old man either, and don't you forget it."

"I didn't say you were frail. I... never mind. Why didn't you answer me?"

"I couldn't hear you with my head under the sink. Why didn't you yell louder?"

"Do you need help with that?" I asked, ignoring his sarcasm.

"No. I'll give it one more turn and, if I can't get the leak to stop, I'll spring for a plumber." He laughed out loud. "Get it, spring for a plumber."

"Yeah, I get it."

Dad gave a final twist on the bolt before standing. He wiped his hands, raised the faucet handle, and watched the water flow. A broad grin spread across his face. No sooner had he said ta-da, then water sprayed from the bolt he tightened.

"Son of a ..." He slammed the faucet handle closed. "Okay, so I won't be supplementing my retirement income as a plumber's aide." He mopped up the small flood with a kitchen towel. "What's this good news you've got?"

"We found the mystery rider."

"Biker chick? James came through then?"

"No, he's still MIA."

"How then?"

"I can't go into specifics. It's a classified program, but we linked James to a parking garage outside of the old outlet mall. It's where he picked up the mystery rider. It took some digging, but we found her. Her name is Sabrina Foster. She lives here in Portland. She's not far from you, actually. She confirmed she spent the evening with him."

"So she was a hooker?"

"No, not like that. She spent a few hours with James the night of the murder. She wasn't a hooker; she was a college student."

"What was James doing with a college student? Did you detain her? Is she in jail now? Does Maxine know?"

"Maxine doesn't know and, no, I didn't arrest her."

"Why the hell not?"

"For one, I'm a civilian."

"You didn't bring the police with you?"

"No, she works in a law firm. I didn't want her to get an attorney before we figured out what she was doing with him."

"You played your hand? What were you thinking?"

The level of fury stunned me. Resentment rose from my gut to meet it. "I thought she would talk freely in her home versus the station."

"Oh yeah, great tactic, and did you pour her a nice spot of tea and give her crumpets while you two went on about her blowing a hole in James' head?"

"I didn't *pour her a spot of tea,* and we didn't *eat crumpets,*" I snapped. I left out that I did, in fact, enjoy a cookie. "Why are you acting like such a jerk? You may not agree, but it worked. She admitted to spending the evening with him, even tying him up, but she's not the killer."

"Right, she tied him up, and someone else came strolling by and shot him? That's your take?"

"Yes. If you would let me finish, I think you'll agree."

I shared every detail of Sabrina's story to include her abuse. Dad sat stone-faced. When I finished, the edge of his ears was fire-engine red.

"How could you fall for that cockamamie story? She's probably halfway to Canada by now," he shouted.

"I didn't fall for anything. She's not halfway to Canada. In fact, she's coming to the station tomorrow to give her statement."

"Sure, she is. I bet you $100 she's a no-show. You should have brought her in and then checked her story out. How could you be so daft? You're as naïve as your mother with your rose-colored glasses seeing the good in everyone."

"Don't talk about Mom. She wasn't naïve. She had as good of instincts as you. I'd rather be like her any day than some bitter-old-coot."

"Give me the damn ex's name. I'll run a background check tomorrow," he said.

This conversation didn't go as imagined. I didn't expect a champagne cork to pop, but I sure as heck didn't expect his head to explode. "I can run it," I snapped back.

"Isn't that my new role in your agency? You've done enough. Let this bitter-old-coot run the damn thing."

The argument sapped my spirit; I gave in.

"Victor Daniels. He lives in Seattle. Or he used to."

"I'll let you know what shakes out," he said.

"Dad, what's going on here? Why can't you trust my instincts? I know Sabrina is not guilty. Why are you criticizing and attacking me?"

"Don't be such a baby girl. I wasn't attacking you. I was pointing out the stupid thing you did."

"No attack there," my voice dripping with sarcasm.

He shrugged. "Maybe I could have been less reactive. We approach things differently. I would have never pulled that stunt. I don't think any detective in his right mind would've."

"It wasn't a stunt; it was a technique to gain her trust."

"I guess we will know tomorrow if it's a technique or a stunt."

"I guess we will."

I headed home. Come hell or high water, I would be at that station tomorrow. I prayed she would show up. I wasn't looking forward to his self-righteous '*I told you so*' if she didn't.

Chapter 11

Even though my intuition told me Sabrina was innocent, Dad was right. She could change her mind, pack up her family, and be halfway to Canada before her scheduled appointment. I wasn't taking any chances. I called Vicky and asked her to check on Cooper and headed over to Sabrina's house.

I parked my car a few houses down from her home with the driveway in plain sight. It would be a long night. I might have dozed for a few minutes here and there but, aside from that, my eyes never left her driveway. I followed her to work the next morning and watched her enter the law office.

Maybe she would bring one of her coworkers with her. I know I would. I leaned back against the headrest, exhausted. Except for a quick coffee and restroom break across the street, I had no intention of leaving the parking lot until I followed her to the station. I looked at my watch. The captain scheduled Sabrina's appointment for 3:00, and it was only noon. Minutes passed like hours.

Fingers crossed, we could keep her confession from the media. There would be no way to put the genie back in the bottle if they found out she was the last person to see James alive. The story wouldn't end with the five o'clock news headline either. They would feature her face on every major magazine and news station across America.

It was almost two when Sabrina and a tall thin man carrying a briefcase walked toward her car. *She's bringing an attorney. Good girl.*

I stayed a few car lengths back as she made her way to the courthouse. The parking lot was full, and they had to park a few streets away. I still had my employee parking pass and entered through the employee garage. I was past security, standing at the elevator, when she entered the building. She waved when she saw me. I felt a pang of guilt for stalking her. I waved back and waited for her to check in through security. She introduced me to her attorney, Marcus Danes.

The elevator opened. Marcus motioned for me to enter first. We both reached for the second floor button.

"You're coming to the interview?" she asked.

"No, I can't."

"Why not?"

"I don't work here anymore. I'm here on another matter." I didn't want to tell her I would be behind a two-way mirror. The captain wanted me to alert him if her story changed in any way.

She reached for my hand. "Please?"

"You'll be fine. I promise. Just tell the truth."

"Will you be here when my interview is over?" she asked. Her voice trembled and sounded like a frightened child, not a stone-cold murderer.

"I'll be here for a few hours. I'm sure you won't take that long. I'll keep an eye out for you."

Her eyes were red and blurry. The bloodshot look that comes from drinking doctored orange juice with her morning toast and no doubt a glass or two at lunch.

I showed them to the interrogation room and swung by the captain's office.

The door was open. I knocked on the frame and stepped in.

"They're all set up," I said.

"They?"

"She brought her attorney, Marcus Danes."

"I don't recognize the name. You know him?"

"I met him in the hall. Honestly, I don't expect he has a criminal law background. More than likely he's a co-worker helping out. I camped at her office this morning. She works for an insurance defense firm. There's nothing to worry about."

"I remember it was in Paul's profile."

"That's right. He gave you a copy."

We split up in the hall. He entered the interrogation room, and I opened the door to the closed-circuit TV viewing room.

I took out my tablet to send him any notes if something seemed off from her original statement.

It surprised me Marcus didn't keep her from talking. He never interrupted. Occasionally, she looked at him for direction, but he always nodded for her to continue. Maybe he had full confidence she wouldn't be a person of interest after her statement. Her account wasn't word for word, but there was no significant deviation from the facts she shared with me. A good sign.

No change would've meant she rehearsed her responses. A complete change in her story suggested she had pondered her story, recognized the holes, and drummed up a more solid alibi. Sabrina didn't need an alibi. She admitted to being there and tying him up. Throughout the statement, she maintained her innocence about the shooting. It was almost 4:30. The interview was long over, but she and Marcus were still in the interrogation room. I sent the captain a note.

Are you done?

He responded. **We are waiting for the fingerprint and DNA tech. Can you find out what's taking him so long?**

It wasn't unusual for the tech to be late by 15 minutes, but 30 was out of the norm. My hand was on the door knob when the captain's phone rang. He walked to the corner of the room, nodded several times, and sat back down. I sent him a note. **Was that the tech? What gives?**

He looked at the camera. He mouthed, I'm sorry.

My fingers flew across the keyboard. **What for?**

The door to the interrogation room opened. Dad walked in with Harold from the DA's office and a police officer.

Harold took charge and motioned for the officer to cuff Sabrina. The officer read Sabrina her rights. Marcus interjected and told her not to say anything else. *Now he's offering advice, after she gave a full interview?*

What was Dad up to? Dad avoided looking at the camera. I sent the captain a note. **Stop this.** He returned, **I can't.**

The officer led Sabrina out of the interrogation room.

I ran into the hall and yelled, "Sabrina."

She turned, eyes wide.

"You promised," she screamed.

She kept screaming at me all the way down the hall into booking.

The captain, Dad, Sabrina, Marcus, and the officer walked into central booking. My knuckles rapped against the door at least a dozen times before the captain finally opened it.

"I can't let you in. You're no longer employed here."

"What's going on? Why is she being arrested?"

He stepped out into the hall. Your dad did a background check on the ex. Her story checked out, but she left out an important detail."

"What detail?

"Her ex reported his .22 caliber pistol stolen the week she left."

"It's a lie Victor concocted. He set her up. He probably reported it stolen because he had every intention of finding and killing her. The stage was set. He could have followed her that night and shot James after she left."

"That's plausible, but we have to arrest her and sort it out," he said.

"Can't you stop this? I promised her no arrest if she came in. Hasn't she suffered enough?"

"The DA is the only one who can press and drop charges. It's out of my hands."

"Are you going to talk to him?"

"I'll try but, face it, Katie, she stole the same caliber of gun used to shoot James."

"So what? It doesn't mean she shot him. There was also a .22 in the safe, and it's missing."

"Why are you so close to this? Why are you such a champion in her defense? It's not like you. Your judgment is clouded. For the life of me, I can't figure out why. Does she remind you of someone?"

His question startled me. "No."

"Something's going on here. Do you relate to her?"

"What do you mean? Was I ever falsely accused of shooting someone in the head?"

"That, right there. That's what I'm talking about. Listen to yourself. You're not even entertaining the idea that she may be guilty."

"Because she's not."

"You're wearing rose-colored glasses. You're not objective. You can't see the holes in her story. I don't mean to pry but, Katie, were you ever in an abusive relationship?"

"No."

"What then? What's making you so protective?"

"I feel she's innocent. I'm certain of it. The same way I'm convinced that... "

"That what?"

"James is deliberately holding back. We need to look at the ex."

"Why?"

"We just do."

"What aren't you saying?" He placed his hand on my shoulder.

I didn't respond but shrugged his hand away.

"Katie, something is making you assume she's not guilty, and don't tell me it's your instinct. What does this woman mean to you? She's triggering something. Don't lie to me; don't lie to yourself."

"It's not why I'm convinced she's innocent, but there is something." My voice dropped.

"What?"

"A stalker murdered my college roommate. It wasn't an ex-boyfriend or even anyone she met, so it's not the same. Justine didn't know who it was. And to make matters worse, there was no proof. There was no tangible evidence like calls, texts, or letters. The stalker kept showing up everywhere she went, staring at her. He tried to talk to Justine a few times but, when she asked him to leave her alone, he snapped. He called her stuck-up and told her he wouldn't let her treat him like that."

"Did she press charges?"

"She reported him to the school and gave a description to the police and even asked the campus cops to watch for him. He seemed to go away for a few weeks but, a month later, he showed up at Pete's Bar on her birthday. She told the bartender he was stalking her, and he kicked him out. Two days later, a student found her strangled in the woods near campus."

"That's horrible."

"Everyone assumes I joined the force to follow in Dad's footsteps, but it was because of Justine. I stood over the grave and swore I would find him and that I wouldn't let anyone live in fear as she did. She couldn't eat or sleep. She couldn't focus, and her grades started to drop. But no one took it seriously. I'm ashamed to say not even me. I called her a drama queen. Those words haunt me. I wasn't supportive. We didn't realize the danger until it was too late."

"So Sabrina reminds you of Justine?"

"Sabrina said Victor could kill. We have to take that seriously. He staged the theft of the gun, knowing he would use it to kill her. He was probably following her and guessed she and James were on a date. He intended to threaten James to never date her again and, when he discovered him tied up, he shot him."

"Katie, admit that it's as likely that the relationship traumatized her, and she overreacted to James not wanting to take her home. She panicked when she hit him over the head. It's possible she stole the gun and had it on her that night. Her adrenaline was pumping. No man would ever hurt her again. She would make certain of it. After she tied him up, her rage against Victor made her snap. She took out the gun and shot him, fearing he would retaliate for her knocking him out. She mentioned several times that he was powerful and feared he would find her. That's why she walked back to her car. Maybe the truth is she killed him and didn't want anyone to see her near his home. She could have made it look like a burglary. You have to admit that's as likely as Victor following her around and killing any man she dated."

He was right. She might have snapped and pulled the trigger yet, every time I checked in with my gut, it didn't ring true.

I needed to talk to P-Kate, and then I had to connect with James.

Chapter 12

I had to run all this by P-Kate. She couldn't tell me if Sabrina was innocent or guilty. But she could share if a stalker murdered Justine in P-Kate's world. If so, did it impair her judgment? I pulled the black stone necklace I received from P-Kate's dimension from my necklace rack, opened my jewelry box, and grabbed the small pyramid she'd given me. Both pieces were made of the same material. I had only used them a few times and hoped it would still work.

I placed them on the dresser and aimed the necklace at the tip of the pyramid. As before, smoke filled my bedroom doorway. I grabbed the pyramid, stepped through, into P-Kate's living room. She was reading a book on the couch with her Cooper pressed against her leg.

I walked over to the couch.

"Can you help me?"

She stood so fast the pup slid off the couch.

"You can't be here. What are you doing?"

"I'm not asking for a case file, just a little help."

She lifted her pants leg. A steady green light emanated from the monitor attached to her ankle. "I'm under house arrest. I can't help you. If I lower my vibration to enter the 3D dimension, it will trigger an alarm."

"What happened?"

"I should never have given you my case file on Sarah. Giving anything more than signs or symbols for you to discern is against the multiverse law. Somehow the Multiverse Task Force got wind of it and arrested me because I showed you who the killer was in my world."

"I thought you were allowed to give signs, symbols, and hints for me to intuit."

"There is a difference between giving nudges and showing you who the killer is. The multiverse law does allow sharing details of possibilities that manifest out of a set of infinite possibilities. However, the laws regarding contact with the 3D world limit the information we can give.

Doppelgängers can't emphasize one probability over another. When I handed you my case file on Sarah, it made you alter the course of your investigation."

"I feel guilty about taking credit for solving the Alexander murder. I wasn't able to tell anyone but Vicky that I was communicating with you."

"Don't feel guilty. You would have solved it. I just sped it up. I couldn't let another person die. If I hadn't intervened, your case would have unfolded the same way mine did. Three families would have died while I waited for you to course-correct on your own."

"Thanks. That makes me feel better. I'm familiar with different dimensions. I wasn't aware the rules were different depending on the dimension."

"The rules are different but can be eased up if the person in the 3D world has raised their vibration and shifted their consciousness to the 5D plane. That was my argument when the task force arrested me. I explained your near-death experience raised your vibration. You had heightened emotions, wanting your Mom and Jimmy back on the day you attempted suicide. Your desire to have your family back together was so strong, you collided with the parallel world holding that probability. That's how we connected. The Task Force agreed on some level, reduced the charges, and placed me on house arrest."

"So the necklace and pyramid brought me to the 5D plane where you live?" I asked.

"You didn't transport anywhere. Your physical body's still in your condo. You shifted your consciousness and opened your heart to the probability of connecting with me. The pyramid and necklace are tools until you can maintain a higher vibration. In time, with meditation, clean living, and intention combined with strong emotions, you'll be able to shift your consciousness and notice me without the tools. You're still in your living room. You're just able to observe me in mine."

"So there is no portal I stepped through?"

"No. You've experienced the shift before. A ton of people in your world have. The astral plane is the 4th dimension. When you leave your body in your dreams and have what resembles real experiences, that's the astral plane. In the astral plane, you have the limitations of the 3rd dimension world. The 5th dimension, 5D, is the next level, where anything can happen by imagining it. Here every reality exists at the same time. With quantum physics, when you have a strong emotion behind your desire, it manifests immediately. You connect with the parallel world where what you desire is more than probable; it has unfolded or will unfold. When you connect with a possibility, a version of you, it brings that vibration into your physical body, and you can manifest your desires."

"I can't manifest bringing Mom and Jimmy back to life."

"No, but you can perceive yourself differently. You can change the way you identify with your past, bring into your cellular memory a beautiful life with them. Let go of the identity of being a twin who lost her brother and mother at an early age. When you dwell on your loss, you stir up heartache and pain. All you can feel is how much you miss them. Instead, identify with the version of you that has a full life with them."

"I have to admit, since colliding with you, I have been happier and more hopeful about my future. I'm even looking at Nick differently. I never had a romantic interest in him. He was always the captain and nothing more. Now that I've felt your love for him and his for you, I can't get him out of my head."

"Have you shared any of this with your Nick?"

"No, I'm confused that I might be reacting this way because you love your Nick, not because I'm falling for mine."

"If it's a probability that resonates with you, go for it. Who cares how it entered your field?"

"My field?"

"You have an energy field that holds your higher self. When you visualize that ideal version of you, it becomes who you are. Let go of trying to control it."

"If you're on house arrest, how did you leave the motorcycle photo on my display?"

"I talked Nick into changing your display."

"The captain broke the multiverse law?"

"We decided it fell under a hint. It was a stretch, but I finally got him comfortable with it."

"I appreciate that. I would never have found Sabrina without it. I'm so sorry I caused you and the captain so much trouble. Are you guys doing okay? I promise I won't ask you to do anything that gets you in any more trouble."

"It was rocky for a while. I'm not going to lie. It was the first time in our marriage that I wasn't candid with him. That's not something he can recover from overnight. I'm earning back his trust, and he will help, but it has to be limited."

"I promise I won't ask you to do anything illegal. You can give me nudges, right? Signs I'm on the right track or that I'm off in left field? You talked Nick into putting the photo on the fridge display, right?"

"Listen—what we did was stretching it. Nick would flip if he knew you were here. It's one thing to manipulate an electronic display, but I'm not going to risk my marriage or his career."

"I won't be but a minute."

She didn't respond but motioned for me to sit.

"Was Justine murdered by a stalker in your world?" I asked.

"Justine? Yes, but why are you bringing up Justine?"

"She may be influencing the Baxter investigation."

"You mean her ghost?"

"No, I may be letting how she died influence how I'm treating Sabrina. Has Justine's murder impacted any of your case files?"

"No, but I'm as haunted by her death as you are. I didn't take her seriously, I thought she was exaggerating for attention. Not taking her stalker serious haunts me. She was beautiful so, of course, guys would stare. I never thought she was in danger."

"I'm being accused of only seeing the good in Sabrina and looking at the case with rose-colored glasses."

"It's not a bad thing to see the world in a pink glow. It doesn't mean you only see the good things. That's a myth. You've seen horrible things over your career. A set of rose-colored glasses can shift your perception and open your eyes in ways you couldn't fathom. I'd hold on to a pair if you've got them."

"Very funny, it's just an expression. It's not literal. I don't actually have a pair."

"Well, the metaphorical glasses might be the prescription you need to solve this case."

I stared at her with my mouth open.

"But, back to Justine—I can tell you she hasn't influenced any of my work-related decisions."

"So my gut is right, Sabrina is innocent. She didn't murder James Baxter. I'm not relating her to Justine."

"You know I can't tell you that," she warned.

"I know, sorry."

"Have you reached James?"

"No. I've tried, but he won't come through."

"That doesn't surprise me. I'm pretty sure he won't help you."

"Is he protecting someone? Why won't he let me help him?"

"Blood is thicker than water."

"It's family, then. Was it Rob?"

"Don't judge a book by its cover."

"Is Sabrina's stalker similar in any way to Justine's?

"You should always take a stalker seriously."

"Her ex shot James?"

"I didn't say that."

"Your hints aren't feeling much like hints."

"The ties that bind are the hardest to break, but that doesn't mean you can't stretch them to the limit."

"What?" *The tie I kept seeing in my dream. Ties that bind.* "I kept dreaming of a tie, that was you?"

We turned toward the kitchen at the sound of the garage door opening.

"He's home. You've got to leave. Just know that people can change. A second chance is worth a second look."

I was in my room. The smoky haze dissipated. I didn't expect answers, but I didn't expect a plethora of riddles either.

What was I to make of all that? *Ties that bind...* That tends to be a reference to family. *Blood is thicker than water* most definitely referred to family. That pulled me back to Rob, but taking stalkers seriously could mean Sabrina's ex was involved. Just like her hints with Sarah, I was getting mixed signals. Too many of the infinite possibilities and not enough answers.

I felt weak. I wasn't sure if I was feeling the effects of the portal or my all-night stakeout. Then there was the late night with Paul and the captain. I needed a cup of coffee.

"Tessa, start a pot of coffee, please."

"I'm sorry, we are out. Shall I place an online order? It can be delivered in a few hours."

"Order a box, and I'll be set for breakfast. For now, I'll grab some at the chain down the street."

"A drone will drop it off in two hours," she responded.

I headed for the coffee chain down the street. The line wasn't too bad. I made my way to the front in short time.

"What are you having?" A less than enthusiastic barista asked. Not the greeting I would get from Mike and Darla's place.

"Tall medium roast with room for cream."

"That'll be $7.50."

I placed my finger print against the reader.

He pulled a cup from the label printer attached to the reader and handed it to a co-worker.

"It'll be at the end of the counter. Next!" he shouted looking over my head.

I stood next to a tall man playing with his phone and waited for my name to be called. Another barista walked over to the counter and held up two large coffees.

"Nick!" he called out.

Nick? Could it be? I glanced around and saw the captain weaving through tables.

"Hi there," I said as he made his way to the counter. He clutched both coffees.

"Well, howdy ho," he returned with a crooked smile.

"I didn't realize you lived on this side of town," I said.

"I don't, I'm..." He turned at the sound of a woman's voice.

"Nick, let's go. I can't be late for class."

A female wearing jeans, an oversized sports shirt, and carrying a backpack raced toward us like a speed-walker. She snatched one of the coffees from him.

I'm not sure she realized we were talking or if she didn't want to squander time on introductions.

"Let's go," she said.

"Ashley, this is Katie, she's one of my detectives, well, until recently anyway."

She tucked her free arm around his, claiming him as her own.

"Hi," she said.

"Hello, nice to meet you."

She yanked on Nick's arm. "Don't mean to be rude, but we've got to run."

Nick spread his stance, firmly planted his feet against the pull, and didn't budge. He took his car remote from his pocket and held it out.

"Grab the car, will you, hon? I'll meet you out front."

"What?"

"It'll only take a minute—just some quick shop talk. I'll be outside before you get there. You won't be late for class, I promise," he added.

She pouted her lips and looked me up and down. "I thought she didn't work for you anymore?"

"We need to wrap up some old business. It'll take a second."

She grabbed the keys and kissed him full on the lips. "You'd better be standing there when I pull up," she threatened as she walked away.

"It was nice to meet you!" I shouted.

She didn't respond but waved her hand in the air. Her fingers had a slight curl. I wasn't sure if that was a goodbye wave or if she was giving me the finger.

I looked back at Nick. "Sorry, I didn't mean to pull you away."

"We have a few minutes. I parked down the road."

"I didn't realize you were a Cowboys fan."

"What?"

"The shirt she was drowning in. I'm assuming it's yours. And she's in school? You know there are laws against that."

"Against what? Oh. It's not what it looks like. Okay, wipe the smirk off your face. It's what it looks like, but she's in college, not high school."

"Did you check her I.D.? It looks like you should read her a bedtime story and tuck her in bed versus…"

"Easy there, she just looks young. She's twenty-six and working on her master's degree. That's why she's carrying the backpack and heading to class."

"Katie!" the barista called out.

"That's my coffee. You'd better not keep your girlfriend waiting. She seems like she has a temper."

"She's not my girlfriend. I mean, it's not defined, not labeled, whatever you call it. We're keeping it light. She's busy with school and work, and I'm, well… you know my focus is the department."

"Great foundation for a long-lasting relationship."

"If I recall, you and Sam were both okay that the job came first."

"Touché."

I grabbed my coffee from the counter and added milk.

After a moment, I said "Sorry, I didn't mean to needle you. I was just surprised to see you with her. She doesn't seem your type."

"And you know my type?"

"I thought I might, but I was way off base."

His voice lowered and he leaned in. "You're not off base. She's not my type. It's just something that's working for now. She wants to keep it light and so do I." He shrugged. "That's all it is. Look, I'm sorry about Sabrina's arrest. I tried to talk to Harold, but he isn't budging. What did your dad say?"

"I haven't talked to him. I can't discuss it with him until I calm down. I feel betrayed and shut out. He should have reached out to me first. When I can think about it without wanting to choke him, I'll talk to him."

"I need to head out, but I'll keep you posted if anything changes. You gonna be alright?"

"Yes, go. She'll tear your limbs off if you make her late for class."

He chuckled. "You call me if you need anything, you hear?"

"I will."

I knew Dad was expecting me to chew him a new one. I was angry, but I couldn't fault him for arresting Sabrina. She was the last one to see James alive; her DNA was on the belt, she had possible motivation and access to a .22 caliber pistol. Whether or not she stole it, there was more than a preponderance of evidence against her. I'd have to talk to him, eventually. I'd might as well invite him to dinner and get us back on track. Furious that he didn't tell me first, I wasn't about to let him off the hook yet.

Chapter 13

I asked Dad to meet me at Rudy's Steakhouse for dinner for two reasons: One, I didn't inherit Mom's love of cooking, and the second was that I wanted to meet in public to make sure things stayed civil. Dad was seated at the bar when I arrived.

"The table's not ready yet," he grumbled.

"That's because the reservation isn't until seven. It's 6:45; we still have 15 minutes."

He handed me a beer.

"Is this a peace offering?" I laughed, trying to lighten the mood.

"I did nothing wrong. All I did was clean up your mess. You're lucky Sabrina didn't take off for Canada."

"Here we go again."

"What's that mean?"

"It means I told you she wouldn't run off. She showed up and gave her statement, didn't she? Did you read it?"

"Yes, I read it, did you catch that she said she never owned a gun?"

"There's no record of her purchasing a gun," I clarified.

"Use your brain. You don't have to purchase a gun to own one. Stealing one from your husband makes you a gun owner."

"Allegedly stole. Have they charged her with his murder?"

"Yes. She's been charged. She admits to being there, her DNA is on the robe tie, and she had access to the same kind of gun."

"The same kind? You don't even have the murder weapon, and you arrested her."

"You know better than anyone— you don't need a murder weapon to charge someone with murder."

"Are you forgetting whoever broke into that safe had access to a .22? That's who killed him. So, which is it? She killed him with her .22 and broke into the safe and thought I kinda like this gun; I think I'll take this one too? How did she know about the safe or that his fingerprint opened it?"

"I guess the DA will have to figure that out."

"Are you refusing to see she's not the killer because you want to be the one to solve the case? I thought you wanted my help."

"You did help. You found Sabrina. I forgot to say thanks for that," he said, taking a swig from his beer.

"What's her bail?"

"We asked for no bail."

"What?"

"She's a flight risk."

"How is she a flight risk? She's a soccer mom who works for a law firm."

"We're about four hours from the Canadian border. She has a passport."

"You've got to be kidding. You're going to let an innocent woman sit in jail until her trial?" My voice was loud enough that the bartender looked our way.

"If you could take those rose-colored glasses off, you'll see she's not as innocent as you think," he said.

"If one more person tells me I'm wearing rose-colored glasses, I'm going to lose my mind."

"You know what your mom always said: if you hear something more than once, it's a message for you."

"That's the second time I've heard that this week."

"You know the next part. If you hear it a few times in a close period, it's a call to action that you can't ignore."

"What's my call to action? To take off glasses I'm not wearing?" I shot back.

I took a few swigs of beer. This dinner was going to need something stronger. I motioned to the bartender.

"Can you get me a shot of whiskey?"

"Make that two," Dad said, holding up two fingers.

"Two whiskeys coming up."

Dad grabbed a coaster and gave it a spin. "What about James? Has he broken his silence?"

"Not yet."

"Gonna ask the captain for your job back since you're no longer connected?"

"No, I'm connected with the other side, just not James."

"What good is it if you can't reach the one you need to talk to?"

"I have another way of reaching him; don't worry about it."

I cringed at the thought. I would to have to cross over and find James. But this time there was no way I would trade souls. After Juliet hijacked my body during Sarah's case, it would be some time before I would trust another soul with my body. I'd have to do this with Vicky so she could watch over my body while I astral projected. Astral projection wasn't as safe as trading souls. A vacant body is open to possession. Then again, swapping souls is only safe if you trust the soul to let you back in. The beeper buzzed and vibrated across the bar, signaling our table was ready. *Saved by the buzzer.* "Let's get our table."

Dad handed the host the unit, and we followed him to our table. It seemed an eternity before the waitress brought our meals. The sound of the forks and knives scraping our plates accentuated the strained silence.

We were halfway through dinner when the hairs on my neck stood up. I felt the familiar cool air across my cheek near my right ear. *Not now*, I thought. Not here. I had an intense sensation of an elderly female and the smell of roses.

"*Hilf ihr,*" I heard in my right ear. *Help her?*

I took a year each of German, Russian, and Spanish in high school. I could tell this was German. I looked around the room to see who the 'her' might be. A young woman, two tables down, sat alone, picking at her food. Her frown deepened as she made her way to the potatoes. She didn't take a bite but continued to play with her food. I watched her for a few minutes.

"*Hilf ihr,*" the voice repeated.

I didn't want to do this in front of Dad and tried to ignore the voice. I sent a mental response. "*Nein, No. Not now, I can't do this now.*"

"*Heute Abend,*" the voice insisted. *Tonight.*

I ignored the plea. The spirit knocked my whiskey glass over spilling the small amount of golden liquid that remained. I pretended that I had bumped the glass when reaching for my fork and placed it upright. I put the few ice cubes left back in the glass. Dad was so busy looking down at his plate, trying not to make eye contact, he didn't react.

I watched as the young lady paid her check. The voice screamed in my head, "*jetzt.*" *Now.*

"*No, Nein,*" I said out loud.

"What?" Dad said. He looked startled at the outburst.

"Nothing."

"Are you drunk?"

Before I could respond, the lady passed our table on her way out.

"*Jetzt!*" The voice screamed in my head again.

Seeing that I was unwilling to help her communicate, she forced her way into my body. She didn't force me out, but she could have. She was strong, on a mission, and wouldn't take no for an answer.

"*Bitte setzen, mein Schatz.*" It came from me, but the voice wasn't mine. I recognized the phrase. *Please sit, my darling.*

She stopped and turned back toward our table.

"Me? You want me to sit down?"

The spirit gave me control but stayed in my body.

I wasn't sure where this was headed.

"Yes, may I have a moment of your time?"

I scooted over in the booth to make room. "*Please sit... setzen,*" I said, patting the seat next to me.

Dad looked at me like I had gone mad.

"What? Why?" She asked.

"I have a message for you. Please sit."

"Do I know you?"

"No. My name is Katie. I know it sounds crazy, but I can communicate with the dead. Please sit. I have a message from an older woman. I think she might be your mother or grandmother. Is there an elderly female that has passed?"

"Both Mom and Oma have passed." She shifted in her seat and looked around.

"I smell roses. Does that mean anything?"

"My Oma, I mean, my grandmother's name was Rose, and Mom named me after her. My name is Rose." She clutched her purse and sat across from me.

I could feel the spirit's frustration and let her come forward. I shifted my consciousness to the background, so her Oma had more control. It was a weird sensation. I understood her thoughts in my mind but also heard them with my ears as she said them. It felt like an echo.

"Deine Kinder brauchen dich, mein Rosenblatt."

"My kids need me, my rose petal?" She repeated in english. "Oma?"

"Oma always called me her rose petal," she leaned in. "Oma, my German is *schlecht,* bad; English please, *bitte.*"

I heard. "Zis too shall pass."

Rose cried, took her phone out of her purse, and showed me the screen saver. It said *this too shall pass.*

"Mom and Oma said it all of the time." She grabbed a napkin from the table and blew her nose. The spirit grabbed Rose's hand. It startled me because it was an automatic reaction, not something she thought before reaching out.

In broken German: "Rose, no babies zar better off wiz out zer mutters. Tare zat goodbye note."

"Oma, I've made a mess of things," Rose cried.

"It's za drugs *mein rosenblatt;* stop za drugs."

"I've tried. I'm not strong like you."

The spirit pleaded with me to help. *Tell her to ignore za bad voices,* she pleaded. I knew all about negative inner dialog, the "bad" voices. I knew exactly what she meant.

I brought my consciousness back to the front, still holding her hand. "I think your Oma is trying to say that when you hear that inner voice that says you're not good enough, tell it to shut up. You're an amazing woman. Tell the voice all the reasons you're good enough. You're a good mother who wants the best for your kids. If you didn't, you wouldn't be thinking of ending your life to spare them watching you waste away from drug abuse."

"I'm in pain; I need the pills!" she cried.

"Rose, I think I can help." I pulled out my business card and handed it to her. "You've got to reach out for help. Reach out to your friends and family for help with the kids. Reach out to agencies for help getting off the drugs. Narcotics Anonymous is a wonderful resource."

She took my card and stared at it a moment before she tucked it in the front pocket of her purse. "I was here tonight to have a last dinner. I was going to make it all go away tonight. The kids are with their dad," she confessed.

"Trust me, I know about suicidal thoughts," I said.

She looked up at me.

"Your Oma is right. No kids are better off without their mom. I grew up without one. I felt so alone not having her to guide me and share in my joyful moments, like graduating from the academy. Or not being there to help me get through the sad moments. Like when I ran from my wedding or when I lost my college roommate. Your kids need you now, and they're going to need you later. Let your love for them give you strength."

She cried and blew her nose.

"I know agencies that can help with rehab and pain management and help with the children. Will you call them if I give you the numbers?"

"Yes."

"Promise?"

"Yes, I promise. Is Oma still here?"

I moved my consciousness back. "Yes, *meine schatz,*" the spirit responded.

"Oma, I'm sorry."

"Get vell mein schatz."

I moved my consciousness forward, then reached over and hugged her for her Oma and me. "Just think of your mom and Oma, and they will be there. She has to go now."

"Ich liebe dich," the spirit said.

"I love you too, Oma. I miss you."

I let go of her and sat back down. I heard *Danka* in my head. It meant thank you. You're welcome, *bitte,* I sent back. I felt the spirit leave.

I leaned back in the booth. "She's gone. Are you going to be all right, Rose?"

"Yes."

"Can I see your phone?" I asked.

She handed it to me without asking why. I dialed my cell phone number. It rang next to me. I opened her contacts, entered the suicide hotline, and handed the phone back. "You have my business card, and you have two numbers here: my cell and the suicide hotline. You call me or the hotline day or night if you feel like hurting yourself. Understand?"

"Got it," she said.

"I have your number now and will send you a text with contact information for agencies that can help you get off drugs and help with the kids."

She got up to leave. "Thank you. You have no idea what this means to me."

"I do." I stood up and gave her another hug. "I need two promises from you: Promise you'll call me or the hotline, and promise you'll reach out to the agencies for help."

"Yes, I promise."

"Yes to both?"

"To both."

"When you pick up your kids tomorrow, hold them tight."

"I will. Thanks." She left, and I sat back down.

I felt like I was in a trance. I had almost forgotten Dad was there.

He stared at me, dumbfounded. "It was the weirdest thing, your face vibrated and I could see an old woman's face vibrating in front of yours. Then it stopped, and your eyes changed to green. I couldn't make out her face anymore, but the voice wasn't yours or sometimes it wasn't yours."

"You might have a little psychic in you. The eyes are the first to imprint," I said.

"Imprint?"

"It happens when I let them in my body. I wasn't going to stream her, but she forced her way in. I'm learning to block them, with Vicky's help, but now I know why she couldn't take no for an answer."

"Does it always work like that?"

"It's a mix. If I'm in a hurry, I can ask spirits to send me the message telepathically, but it's usually broken words or symbols. The message is clearer if I let them share my body. Sharing the body is like the channeling you see in movies. Then there is streaming. It's another form of channeling, clearer messages, but more drastic because I have to leave my body and give the spirit full access. I've only done that a few times. Not sure I'm willing to do that again. It's pretty intense."

"You, you, just saved that woman's life," he stammered. He wiped at a tear with the back of his hand.

"Her grandmother, her Oma, did. I just facilitated."

"I'm sorry I doubted you when you couldn't reach James and I wasn't there for you when Jimmy and your mom died. I didn't think about how alone you were. Can you ever forgive me?"

I placed my hand on his. "I already have."

"You carry the suicide hotline number with you? Are you still having suicidal thoughts?"

"No. I'm never going to do that again."

"Please be honest. I get that you never want to talk about your suicide attempt. I want to trust you when you say you have no intention of doing that again, but I can't think that's something you can just shut off. Would you tell me, Vicky, or call the suicide hotline if the suicidal thoughts reoccur?"

"I will say something if that happens. I promise."

"I wish your mother would have said something, and I would have paid closer attention to her. I can't lose you too."

I didn't know if it was the worry on his face, the tremble in his voice, or if I needed to say it out loud, but I confessed it wasn't a spontaneous decision to end my life.

"I've always carried the suicide hotline with me ever since I was a street cop. I'm surprised you don't."

"In my day, we didn't focus on mental health; a crime was a crime. You got locked up, did your time, and you got out to repeat the same thing over again. We missed a big component of breaking the cycle and getting to the root of it. There was media hype that departments were providing sensitivity training, but most of us didn't attend or didn't take it seriously. Are you *sure* that's the only reason you still carry it? To pass it on if you think someone needs it? Why didn't you use it that night?"

"You're right. I've been having suicidal thoughts since I was a kid, and it's difficult to shut it down. It's under control. I'm focused on this second chance and, although it still scares the crap out of me to talk to ghosts, it also inspires me. I'm excited by all the good it'll do. Giving the deceased closure, giving loved ones closure and, fingers crossed, having a chance at locking away the murderer keeps me grateful that I'm still here."

"Do you think it was because your mom killed herself that you tried?"

"It started before her suicide but intensified after she died. I remember after Jimmy died, lying in bed wishing that I was old enough to drive so I could drive the car off a cliff or into a tree."

His eyes brimmed with tears. "Thank heavens you were too young to drive."

I gave him a weak smile and continued. "I did this for a year or so until one day I read a book about a young girl cutting her wrists. In the book, a priest came to visit her in the hospital and told her it was God's blessing she was still alive. He told her to never try it again. If she were successful the next time, her soul would stay in limbo through eternity. She wouldn't be in heaven or hell, just this black void. I recall wondering, 'is that true? How horrible.' It's the only reason I stopped daydreaming about killing myself. When I got older, stressed out, and sleep deprived, the thoughts surfaced again. I always played Russian roulette with my revolver on the anniversary of their deaths, but it never went off. I saw the pills in the drawer and thought it was a sign. I wasn't thinking straight."

His face went white at the revelation that I played spin the chamber every year.

"Why didn't the fear of being stuck in limbo stop you that night? Why didn't you call the hotline?"

"I just wanted it to stop. Even if I had remembered how afraid I was of eternal limbo, it's like my brain got stuck on a track. I couldn't see any reason not to do it. I never even thought about the hotline."

"You said you had it under control. Do you still have thoughts about killing yourself?"

"I'm not sure they are my thoughts or just my brain repeating an old tape."

"For instance?" he asked.

"Sometimes when the alarm goes off, I think out of habit, when I first wake up and my eyes open, a little voice says *'Damn I'm still here.'* It's not often but, when it happens, I say *'Cancel, cancel. Yes, damn, I'm still here!'*"

"I love it, erase that old tape," he said.

"It's like a cut and paste. Highlight the old thought and paste in the new one. Over time, all you have is the new one and the old track gets filled in. At least I think that's how the psychiatrist described it. I just know it's working."

"I'm here for you," he said.

"I'm fine. I promise I'll call if I start to spin out."

He reached over and hugged me. It felt foreign but comforting.

Chapter 14

Cooper was tail-wagging happy when he greeted me at the door. Too tired to take him for a walk, I turned on the porch light and threw his favorite ball a few times before settling in. My plan was to curl up with my favorite book, a warm fire, and put the day behind me.

I texted Rose goodnight and sent the contact numbers of the agencies that help get addicts clean. I washed my face and was holding my toothbrush when the hair on my neck and arms stood up as cool air caressed my cheek. Cherry tobacco assaulted my nostrils. The temperature dropped.

"James?"

No response.

"It's time to step up, James."

This was beyond frustrating. "James, are you aware Sabrina is in jail for your murder?"

"She's where she belongs. She tied me up and she is the reason I'm dead."

Finally, he was willing to talk. "Sabrina admits that she tied you up, but she says she didn't kill you."

"She did this to me."

I considered all the references to rose-colored glasses. James was straight up, saying she killed him. Why didn't that ring true in my gut?

"James, she didn't mean to hurt you. It scared her when you wouldn't take her home. She swears you were alive when she left. You could've been unconscious and didn't witness your killer. It might be her ex-husband. Did you see a man in the house or a man watching at the park?"

Silence.

"James? Was anyone following you that night?"

"She did this to me," echoed through the bathroom.

Cooper gave a low growl seconds before the mirror shattered. I dropped my toothbrush in the sink and stepped back. I wasn't sure if the next step would be him sending shards of glass at me. I looked at my jigsaw puzzle reflection.

Cooper barked a few times, leaned against my leg, and backed me out of the bathroom. He relaxed once we were out but stayed at my hip. Although the stink of tobacco lingered, Cooper's body language told me James had left.

I was thrilled he finally reached out. The lack of detail surrounding his murder frustrated me. I wasn't mad about the mirror and could understand his aggravation. His accusation was explicit. Sabrina killed him, and it angered him that I wasn't on board.

I could no longer ignore the fact that she may have committed the murder. P-Kate's comment not to judge a book by its cover nagged at me. Was Sabrina outwardly the girl next door, capable of killing?

Reading was out of the question. Why did P-Kate say it wasn't a terrible thing to wear rose-colored glasses? Was there some dual meaning? She wasn't suggesting that I examine past events in an unrealistic positive light, was she? Perhaps it was about the color rose and not the glasses.

"Tessa, research the color rose."

"Rose is the color between red and magenta."

"Anything special about magenta or red?"

"You need red and blue to make magenta."

Okay, not helpful. I needed to be more specific.

"What does wearing rose-colored glasses mean?"

"Not based in reality, not accepting the negative," she responded. "Optimistic view, unwarranted," she added. "You only acknowledge the good in people, making your view unrealistic," she continued. "Shall I use it in a sentence?"

"No, no. I get it. You don't have to beat me over the head with it."

"Ah, overly emphasized, rubbing it in, got it."

"Tessa, what else do you have on wearing rose-colored glasses?"

"Rose-tinted glasses decrease migraines."

"What? How?"

"They block the flickering blue from fluorescent lights and computer screens. This can be a trigger for migraines and eye strain."

The color had a deeper meaning that wouldn't be on the internet. I needed to run this by Vicky. She was an expert on the energy of colors and spiritual implications. P-Kate was providing this clue and, for the life of me, I couldn't figure it out.

Chapter 15

Because I no longer had my homicide badge, Sabrina had to place me on a visitor's list. It surprised me she agreed to meet with me. Shame washed over me. I hated to admit that this was my first visit since her arrest.

The process took much longer as a civilian. I had to show two forms of ID, run my purse through the X-ray machine, and wait in line for the staff to run a wand across my body even though I had just walked through the body scanner. I chewed on James' words while I waited in line. He never said Sabrina killed him; he just said she was the reason he was dead.

They released me to enter the first set of doors. The clank behind me always made me feel a little claustrophobic. The second set opened to the public area of the jail. I moved to the cube that showed Sabrina on a closed-circuit TV. Our video conference was active. Sabrina had two black eyes and one swollen shut. She had a large cut on her upper lip. I opened the app from my phone and activated the audio, and placed my wireless earbuds in my ear.

"What happened to you? Are you okay? Did they take you to the clinic?"

She cried and repeated the words that still rattle through my mind. "You promised they wouldn't arrest me. You tricked me."

"I didn't trick you. It's my dad's fault."

"Your dad? Who is your dad, and why would he want me arrested?"

"He was the original detective assigned to James' murder." When I told him I found you and shared your story, he ran a background on your ex. He discovered Victor reported his .22 caliber gun stolen the day after you left. Victor accused you of stealing it the night you ran away. It's the same caliber gun used on James."

"My lawyer told me, but I swear I didn't steal Victor's gun. I didn't shoot James."

"I want to believe you, but James told me you were responsible for his death. I can't stay in your corner if you lie to me. If he was trying to rape you and you killed him, it's self-defense, but not if he was tied up. I get you were scared, but you were no longer in danger once you tied him up. We can work with what happened. It's understandable if you went into a rage with all you had been through with Victor. You can plead temporary insanity. Has your lawyer talked to you about your defense?"

"I didn't lose my mind. I didn't shoot him," she insisted.

Her eyes narrowed and she looked me square in the eyes. "Wait, what do you mean, James told you? He's dead."

"I crossed over after a near-death experience. I can communicate with the dead. I've been trying to channel James for months, and he just recently came through and told me you were responsible."

She pushed her chair back as though she was going to stand and end our visit. "Are you trying to trick me into a confession? I thought you were on my side."

"No tricks, I'm on your side. Sabrina, you have no reason to trust me, but please believe me."

"If what you're saying is true, I can't even guess why he is lying or why he thinks I shot him. Maybe he was still unconscious when Victor came in and shot him, and he thinks it's me," she offered.

"I think Victor filed the report of the missing gun with the full intention of killing you. I'm sure he followed you that night and intended to rough James up after you left. When he saw James tied up, his rage at you leaving him and dating someone else led him to shoot James. I just need to prove it."

"We weren't dating."

"From his perspective, you were. Perhaps he saw the two of you leave the garage and followed you. It looked like a date. You spent hours together, watched the sunset, and ended up at James' house."

"If he followed us, it *is* my fault he is dead!" she cried. "But I don't deserve to be in jail."

"I agree, Victor is the one who belongs here. Is there anything you can tell me about the night you left, about the gun? Anything about Victor that would show he's capable of doing this?"

"I have two police reports on record. I never told my friends what was happening, and my parents are dead. They are the only ones that could have testified to his behavior. I'm screwed. I'll die in prison."

"You're not using the lawyer you brought when you gave your statement, are you? He may not be the best one if he doesn't have a criminal background."

"No. He was just a friend helping me out. I trusted you and didn't hire a criminal attorney. A decision I'll regret for the rest of my life."

I had no words.

"Who did you hire?"

"Max Goldberg."

"I have experience with him. You're in excellent hands."

She pushed her chair back and stood up. The lower half of her body was visible on the TV.

"Please sit, tell me what happened to your face? Who did this to you?"

She sat back down. "What does it matter? If I tell, someone will hurt me for being a snitch."

"I can pull some strings and get you put in solitary confinement or have you put on light duty like working in the jail library. That should keep you out of the general population for a few hours a day."

"I won't be in solitary confinement forever, and special favors will just make it worse. Please don't help me."

"I feel responsible. I want to help."

"You *are* responsible." She stood up and lowered her headset.

"Sabrina, wait."

She held her hands in front of her, a signal to the guard she was ready to be cuffed and returned to her cell.

Chapter 16

Vicky agreed to meet me for coffee at Mike and Darla's. She was as hooked on their pastries as I was. When I arrived, she had blueberry scones for each of us and Vicky's favorite, a peppermint mocha latte.

"Sorry to drag you out in this weather."

"I'd never leave my house if I waited for pleasant weather. But this rain is getting old," she said.

"Try walking a dog in it. Nothing like the smell of a wet dog."

"Okay, you beat me. I'll stop complaining. Sounds like you have significant progress. You reached James and P-Kate."

"I wouldn't call it progress. James said that Sabrina killed him."

"That's great. Sabrina killed him, and you have her in custody! Why the long face? We should be celebrating."

"I visited Sabrina yesterday. My gut tells me she's innocent."

"What did P-Kate say?"

"Her usual riddles. She encouraged me to get a pair of rose-colored glasses to open my perception."

"This makes so much sense."

"Buying a pair of rose-colored glasses?"

"Yes."

"You might be kidding. However, it turns out they are available. I thought wearing glasses was symbolic, but I searched the internet and found a few pairs. They are used to help with migraines and for blocking the blue light emanating from electronic screens," I said.

"Wild."

"What?"

"Red and blue make magenta."

"That's what Tessa said. So?"

"That is the color of the 8th Chakra. You've got the grounding red root Chakra and the blue throat Chakra. Red represents life force energy and the will to survive. Blue represents truth and spirituality. Blending the two takes root/grounding/reality with truth and spirituality, creating magenta, which is the color of the 8th Chakra!"

"I thought there were only seven Chakras."

"There are seven within the physical body. The spiritual body has around a dozen. These are a few feet above the head."

"You're excited by this, but I'm not making the connection."

"Rose is a shade of red. When you add the spirituality and innocence of white to red you get pink. You get pink rose-colored glasses."

"You're going to need to spell it out for me."

"Magenta is the color of the 8th Chakra. It's the first spiritual Chakra. It holds all your karma from each lifetime. It's the Akashic library for your soul's contract, your life's purpose. You've got the grounding/reality of the red root Chakra on one spectrum, and the spirituality, life's contract of magenta on the other end of the spectrum, and rose is smack dab in the middle as a bridge between the two. That's why P-Kate said it's a good thing to wear rose-colored glasses and that it opens your perception. White spirituality added to grounding red shifts the perception from material to spiritual. People with rose-colored glasses aren't just focusing on the good and blocking out the negative. They understand that both the good and negative are agreed-upon life contracts. This lets them let go of the events that most people hold on to. It's not about being naïve. It's about understanding the agreements made before a person incarnates," Vicky said in one breath.

"Ah, so James agreed he would be shot in this lifetime. That's why he doesn't want to help. Being murdered was his life contract."

"You got it! Look at this murder from a life contract perspective. Usually, something as intense as murder is tied to your core group. These are spouses, children, and parents. His spouse died of cancer before James was murdered. Both the son and daughter were persons of interest. Rob was out of the country, but that doesn't mean he couldn't have hired someone. Maxine has a partial alibi. Just because Sabrina's DNA is on the robe tie doesn't mean Maxine isn't involved."

"How does wearing the glasses move us forward in the case?"

"It might activate your 8th Chakra which is the connection to everything spiritual or it could be tied to blocking out the blue light. We need a pair to test this out."

"Where are you going with blocking out the blue light?" I asked.

"Most people report ghost sightings at night, so spirits must be visible in a specific light spectrum. The twilight-blue sky goes away at dark, and the spectrum of light without the blue allows people who are not psychic to see ghosts. It's just a thought."

"We can test it on me. I can only hear spirits. You think if I block the blue light, their image will come through? If your theory is correct, why aren't they visible when my room is dark?"

"It may have something to do with the rose color remaining and the blue extracted," she said.

I pulled out my phone and ordered a set online. Vicky could see spirits, so she would be able to help me validate what I saw. I placed the phone down.

"My glasses will be here by 10:00 am."

"Where shall we meet to test them?" she asked.

"There is an intersection downtown that has numerous accidents. A large number of drivers report that something jumps out in front of their car, causing them to swerve and crash. When they inspect, there is nothing there. It could be a ghost or several ghosts. I can't remember the name of the street. It's the one in front of the old bookstore and the second-hand furniture store," I said.

"Right, I'm familiar with the area you're talking about," she said.

"Let's meet at the bookstore at sunset. The glasses blocking out the twilight sky could be the perfect blend," I said.

"Possible," she said.

My smile dropped into a frown. "I'm not sure if putting a face to the voices will make me more comfortable communicating with spirits or make it scarier. Do they ever show up like the moment they died? Head split open or face torn off from an accident or gunshot?" I've seen some gruesome stuff in my years as a homicide detective, but I'm not sure I'm ready for that."

"They *can* show up like they were at the moment of death. Some do it for shock effect, some because they haven't realized they have passed and are stuck. Just like your request for no contact between bedtime and when you wake, you can ask them to appear whole. Most will honor it, especially since you're willing to help them."

"No peeled faces, please!" I shouted out with a hoot.

A couple at the table next to us looked at me like I was crazy.

Vicky burst out laughing.

Chapter 17

I arrived early because I was excited to test my new glasses. The bookstore had a few worn chairs and small tables under the overhang outside the front entrance. I thumbed through a few used books on a rack next to the chairs. Nothing grabbed my attention. I plopped down on one of the chairs and put on my glasses. The intersection was a few feet to the right. The sun was setting when Vicky sat down next to me.

"See anything yet?" she asked.

"Not yet. You?"

"I do, but it's not a ghost. It's an imprint. You may need to get closer."

"An imprint?"

"You remember, imprints are not spirits but a recording of a repeated pattern."

"Right, I learned that in the group. The example used was a wife who roamed the halls, looking out the window towards the sea for her lost husband. Her heightened emotions during the repeated pattern caused emotionally charged energy to be recorded in the ethers. It left an imprint that some people can pick up on. People think they're witnessing her ghost, but they're seeing the imprint of her repeated pattern. So what imprint are you seeing?" I asked.

"We need to get closer to the intersection," she instructed.

I put on my glasses and lifted myself out of the comfy sofa using the armrest and walked over to the intersection. There was little light left in the sky.

"Do you know the last time there was an accident here?" I asked.

As if on cue, a car swerved as if avoiding something and was T-boned by another car.

The impact jammed the driver's side door shut, preventing him from exiting. I called 911 and ran to the passenger side.

"Stop trying to get out. Stay still. The paramedics need to examine you before you move," I said.

I opened the front passenger door and sat next to him.

"What happened?" I asked.

"Crazy cyclist jumped in front of my car. They want you to share the road with them, but most refuse to obey the traffic laws. They weave in and out of traffic like they own the road. Where did he go? Did I hit him?" he asked.

At that moment I was still wearing my glasses and saw a car hit a male cyclist crossing the street; a female cyclist stood on the corner, screaming. She threw her bike down and ran into the intersection and threw her body onto the cyclist. Traffic moved slowly around our car and rolled through the cyclists, oblivious to their presence. The scene repeated over and over.

Vicky leaned into the car window. "You okay, sir? The ambulance is on the way."

"I'm okay. How's the other diver? Where's the guy on the bike? Did that son of a … take off? I'll sue him when I find him."

I made eye contact with Vicky and motioned to the right of the car, letting her know I could see the imprint unfolding. She nodded.

The ambulance pulled up. Carlos, the EMT who saved me after my suicide attempt, exited the rear of the ambulance and headed to the other driver. When he saw Vicky, he motioned for his partner to check on the other driver and walked over to us.

"Vicky? Were you in the accident?"

"No. I'm okay."

Carlos came to the passenger side. "Katie? Are you injured?" He looked at the driver. "Sir, are you okay?"

I stepped out of the car.

"I'm good. Just keeping him company until the ambulance got here. We were at the bookstore across the street when it happened."

"Thank heavens," he said.

He took my place in the passenger seat.

"What's your name, sir?"

"Philip. Can you get me out of here?"

"Let me examine you first. Are you experiencing any pain?"

"My back and my neck, but it's not bad."

Carlos completed his exam and placed a brace around Phillip's neck.

"If you move, I can crawl out of the passenger side," Phillip said.

"Stay still, sir, " Carlos responded.

"I'm fine, really, just sore."

"The fire department is on its way. They'll open your door with the Jaws of Life and get you on a stretcher from the driver's side."

"Jaws of Life? I'm just sore."

"It's best to move you from the driver's side since you're experiencing pain. Hang tight," Carlos assured him.

He stepped out of the car and hugged me.

Vicky came around to the passenger side and hugged Carlos.

"Hello, how is my favorite knight in shining armor?" she asked.

"Fine. How is my favorite psychic?"

"Get a room," I teased.

Carlos blushed.

"Did you see what happened?" he asked.

"He said he swerved to miss a cyclist, but I didn't see the bike until after the accident," I said.

"Where is the cyclist now? Any injuries?"

"He's technically not here," Vicky chimed in.

"Did he flee the scene? Um, you said technically..."

"The cyclist was not in this timeline."

"You can see his ghost? Is this ghost the reason so many accidents happen here?"

"I thought you didn't believe I could see spirits," Vicky said.

"I admit when we dated, you constantly walking up to total strangers to give them a message from a dead relative freaked me out. I know you have a gift. I'm sorry I couldn't handle it and bailed. So, can you send the cyclist to the light?" he asked.

"Thanks. I appreciate that. I'm sorry you bailed, too." Vicky took a deep breath. "It's hard to explain, but it's not a ghost. It's an imprint."

"Well, send the imprint to the light," he said, motioning to the sky.

"It's an energetic pattern. You can't interact with it. It's a recording in time. Similar to the way some pottery pieces have been found to record snippets of sound in the room when the pottery wheel is spinning."

"I'm not sure what you're talking about, but how do we get rid of it?"

"We can't," she said.

"Why can't we?" I interjected.

"I just told you. It's an imprint. You can't interact with it. It's not a spirit you can talk into walking into the light."

"If it's a recording like pottery, you can break the pottery. Right?" I asked.

"Sure."

"Why can't you break the imprint? If I understand you correctly, it's stuck energy. We need to dissipate the energy and break the pattern and make it disappear," I said.

"How do you propose we do that?" she asked.

"I have an idea, but I'll need one of you to do it," Carlos said, reaching into his trauma bag. He pulled out two pen-sized defibrillators and handed them to Vicky. "I can't see the whatever you called it, so you need to do it."

"Do what?" she asked."

"Break up the energy," he said.

I realized what he intended the moment Vicky asked. He was going to shock it.

"We need to hit the pattern with the defibrillator pens and break up the imprint," I said.

Vicky handed me the pens. "Do you want the honor? This intersection was your idea."

I took the units. "How do I use them?"

"Hold them about an inch apart. Put your thumb on the top of each and press down when you get to the ghost. They are already holding a charge. If you need to go a second round, twist the bottom of each for a few seconds and twist back."

"When you get to the imprint," Vicky corrected.

"Imprint." Carlos rolled his eyes.

The fire department arrived. Carlos motioned for them to go to the driver's side.

While the fire department worked on extracting Philip, Carlos stopped traffic so I could walk into the intersection.

I walked up to the energetic recorded image playing out in a loop. The woman was crying over the man's body. When I got to the intersection, the recording started over. I zapped the image at the same moment the driver hit the cyclist. It froze for a brief moment, and then the cyclist's body vibrated before disappearing. I reset the charge and hit the woman's image as she crossed the intersection. I walked back to the car and handed Carlos the units.

"It worked. That was cool," I said.

Vicky held out her hand. "Carlos, can I have them?"

I looked at Carlos. He nodded.

"Do you see another imprint?" he asked.

"No, but I'd like to borrow them for a few hours. Is that possible?"

"My partner has another set so, yes, it's possible. Those may look small, but they come with a big price tag. Don't lose them. It's more than a year's salary for me. What are you going to use them for?" he asked.

"I want to take it to a crime scene."

"What crime scene?" I asked.

"The Baxter mansion," she said.

"We can't just ring the doorbell and walk in. I'm not a detective anymore. We'll need to schedule an appointment. Give Carlos the units back, and we can reach out to him once we have it scheduled."

She handed Carlos the defibrillator with a pout. "I'll be coming back for those."

He held one of the pens up and winked. "Looking forward to it."

Chapter 18

I was about to pull into the driveway when my phone rang. Maxine's name and number flashed on the navigation pane. I had left several messages with her secretary and a few on her cell, letting her know I was new to the case and wanted to walk through the house as part of my investigation. It had been a few days, so it surprised me she returned my call.

"Answer call." The Bluetooth icon of a phone with the handset off popped up next to Maxine's name. "Maxine, thanks for returning my call."

"This is Carol, Maxine's assistant. She's asked me to reach out to you. She cannot accommodate your request to inspect her home. She remodeled the house and doesn't see the point."

"Can you put my call through? I'd like to talk to her to explain the point."

"That's all the information she provided. Her schedule is tight. She has no openings for a call. Please discontinue your attempts to reach her."

"I'll be quick."

"You have her answer. Good day."

The call dropped. The icon and contact info disappeared.

I hit the center steering wheel with my fist. The horn blared, causing me to jump. Crap, I needed to get into that house. I wasn't confident that I would see an imprint, but had to try. If the killer shot James when he was unconscious, maybe his death wouldn't have recorded. If he was alive and knew he was about to die, his emotions may have caused an imprint. Getting into the house was the only way I could know for sure.

I'd have to revert to Plan B. Carol asked me not to call again, but that doesn't mean Dad can't. Maybe he could convince Maxine. He could say he'd reopened the case and needed to bring me up to speed. He could tell her it is his idea to walk me through the home to refresh his memory.

"Call Dad."

He picked up on the first ring. "What's up?"

"I'd like to run an idea by you. Can I stop by?"

"Can't you tell me now?"

"It's a favor I'd like to ask in person."

"I'm just as likely to say yes or no on the phone."

"It's something I'm pretty sure you'd be against. I'd like to throw my pleading eyes into the mix," I laughed.

"If you're trying to sway me, it will cost you a burger and fries."

"Deal. I'll throw in a shake and see you in ten."

"Door's unlocked. Just walk in."

I threw the car in reverse and headed to the drive-thru closest to Dad's.

Dad was sitting on the couch when I walked in. He got up and followed me to the kitchen. "That smells great."

I pulled the burger and fries out of the bag. "You think the burgers smell great, wait till you get a load of this," I held up a large shake up like it was the holy grail.

He laughed, "Is that chocolate?"

"Is there any other kind?"

"Not in my eyes. That must be some favor you want. You're really buttering me up here."

"It's a small favor."

"Spill it," he said as he took a long draw on the straw.

"I called Maxine to see if she would let me in the home. I wanted to see if I could get any images or feelings from the murder scene. She wouldn't even take my call. She had her secretary shoot me down. I was hoping you would convince her."

"I won't." His voice had a hard edge to it. "Why would you dredge up painful memories for her? You have the murderer in jail. What's the point?"

"The point is we have the wrong person in jail."

"Not that nonsense again," he said.

"It's not nonsense. We need to be able to disagree on a case and still move forward with the investigation."

"You mean we need to disagree on a case and let you continue to run down the rabbit hole, pulling everyone in with you."

"I'm not running down the rabbit hole. There were two .22 caliber guns. There was one gun in the safe and *allegedly* one stolen by Sabrina when she left her husband. Both guns need to be run down as probable murder weapons. You can't stop investigating because one of two possibilities surfaces. On that note, we never found Sabrina's gun, so maybe it's not the murder weapon. The only way to rule it out is to find the Baxter .22 that was in the safe."

"The murder weapon isn't in the home. We searched every inch of the place."

"I know that. I want to see if I can get a reading on the crime scene. James might be more willing to help if I'm in the room where the murder took place."

"How am I going to tell her you want her dad's ghost to come screaming down the halls?" he asked.

"Streaming," I said.

"What?"

"It's 'streaming' her Dad, I don't want him to come screaming down the halls. I want to channel him," I said.

"Streaming, screaming, it still involves telling her you want to contact her dad. Need I remind you he hasn't been willing to help? What makes you think that will change because you're standing on the spot where he died? Do you think it will remind him he's dead? I'm pretty sure he's looped into that fact."

"It doesn't matter if he doesn't come through. I don't need James. His imprint will tell the story," I said.

"His what?"

"I was hoping to see the imprint of his murder."

"Is his ghost an imprint?"

"No. I learned a new technique today. If an event repeats enough times, an energetic recording or image is left behind. I know how to see the pattern now."

"James was only shot once. How could he have left a pattern?"

"It's not just when a person repeats an emotionally charged behavior. It can happen with an intense event such as a murder or witnessing a murder."

"You can see this even after 20 years?"

"Yes. The recording stays in the energetic field forever. I saw the imprint of a cyclist get run over today, and his wife or girlfriend was a witness. The imprint could have resulted in her horror of seeing the event."

"You think Sabrina saw the murder and she caused an imprint?"

"That or James caused the imprint. It's a long shot, but I'd like to try."

He crossed his arms. "Sounds crazy."

"I'm not sure why you're fighting me every step of the way. You asked me to take this case. *You* approached me, not the other way around. You wanted me to use my psychic skills because every single clue you tracked down was a dead end."

"Take it easy. I'll do it. I'm not sure of the best way to approach Maxine. Let me think about it."

"Even if the imprint isn't there, the murder site could be the best place to stream James and get the full story. Hearing from James or seeing the imprint would settle our dispute over Sabrina."

"Okay, okay."

"You're still coming by the office tomorrow to look at the set up, right?"

"I'll be there."

Chapter 19

Dad's office was furnished from the last tenant but needed a fresh coat of paint. He walked in as I laid out sample paint strips across his desk.

I picked one up and held it against the wall.

"Vicky recommends khaki. She said it complements the mahogany furniture."

"Cut out the pretense of decorating my office. I know you only care about my conversation with Maxine."

I dropped the sample to my side. "So, can I see the house?"

"No."

"Why not? How hard did you try?"

"I didn't put the screws to her if that's what you mean," he snapped.

"Why not?"

"With the renovations, not a stitch is left of the original crime scene. The inspection would serve no purpose other than dredging up painful memories."

"Our inspection…" I paused, letting my tone sink in. "It was about streaming James. We weren't expecting a chalk outline with a broken vase next to it. You know that. Why didn't you fight for me?"

"When I told her about Sabrina's arrest a few weeks ago, she went on about how grateful she was; I kept my promise to find her father's murderer. Yesterday, she apologized there was nothing left of the crime scene, and she seemed overly devastated there was nothing she could do to help. Maxine said she was confident Sabrina would spend the rest of her life in jail with no intervention on her part."

I stood with my arms crossed. "Unbelievable. Thanks for going all out."

"You're welcome. I did."

"You did what?"

"I went all out."

"In what way?"

He took a paper from his jacket pocket and handed it to me. "Call Rob."

I looked at the paper. It was a handwritten note with *ROB* in all caps and *cell* written next to a phone number. "Why am I calling Rob?"

"He's co-owner of the home. James left the mansion to both Maxine and Rob. He never moved back in, but still owns half. Maybe he'll give you permission."

"I'm confused."

"It was the shift in Maxine. She bent over backward, trying to find her dad's murderer during the investigation. Now we have a person in custody, her response is 'good luck with that?' That didn't sit well with me, so I double-checked to see if Rob was still an owner."

"Why didn't you start with that?"

"There wasn't time. You jumped down my throat as soon as I said you couldn't see the house."

"I'm sorry. Thanks. You're the best." I grabbed the desk phone and pushed it to the center. "Can you start the conversation? Wait, doesn't he hate you for suspecting him? Why would he help?"

"He's not my biggest fan, but he doesn't hate me. After he turned his life around, we had a lot of heart-to-heart talks. He knows why we suspected him and didn't blame me. At least I hope it's still the case."

"Great. You start. I'll jump in after the niceties." I hit the speaker button on the phone's console, dialed, and motioned for Dad to sit.

Dad sat and leaned in close to the speaker.

"Hello."

"Rob? Hello, it's Detective Hanson."

"Jim? How the hell are ya? What's going on?"

"Yeah, it's Jim. Sorry I've been such a stranger. I think about you and Maxine all the time. I'm a schmuck for letting so much time pass. You doing all right?"

"Don't sweat it, brother. We're all busy doing our own thing. I'm good. Trying for the work-life balance, but falling short. Work's sucking the life out of me. You?"

"Glad to report I'm retiring soon. That's why I'm calling. I'm passing your dad's case to my daughter, Katie. She's just hung up her detective hat and has shifted to the private sector as an investigator. I wanted to put the two of you in touch. She's here now."

"Hi, Rob, nice to meet you. Sorry for your loss. I'm hoping I can make a shift in the case and am excited about a recent development. Has Maxine talked to you at all about our recent break in the case?"

"No, we run different parts of the company and rarely reach out these days. Did you find out who murdered my father?"

Dad nodded. "I should have called you. My bad. I figured Maxine would fill you in. We made an arrest!"

"You're kidding. I'll smack my sister for not telling me. I know we're both busy, but this is huge."

I glared at Dad. "Sorry, Rob, we didn't mean to get your hopes up. My dad should've started with 'we think she is innocent, but are hoping she can give us some clues that can get us to the murderer.'"

"What clues?"

"The woman we arrested was at the house the night of the murder. She's the one who tied him up, but swears he was alive when she left."

"That doesn't make any sense."

"Would you mind if we finished the discussion in person? I was hoping, maybe at the house, so I can do a walkthrough? I know it's revamped, but I've got a weird sixth-sense kind of thing going and just want to get my vibe."

Dad rolled his eyes.

"Vibe? Psychic stuff?"

"Uh, not psychic, per se, but I'm picking up some skills from a psychic friend. Hard to put it in words."

"The wife's into it. Don't always get it when she talks 'I'm getting, I'm feeling' stuff, but I'm not against it. It shouldn't be a problem; get with Maxine and let me know the time. I'll meet you both there. It will be an opportunity to catch up with her."

"Well… that's another reason we are reaching out to you. Maxine passed on my request to come to the house. She didn't want to dredge up painful memories, I think. Would you mind setting it up? We can go together if it's easier. It'll let us catch up in the car, so we won't bring up painful memories in front of Maxine. Or perhaps we can schedule it when she's at work, and you can just give me a tour of the house. Low-key-like."

He gave a slow whistle. "That changes things. My sister's pretty set when she makes her mind up. We haven't been on the best terms since our dad died. I think she has always had doubts about my role in it."

Dad winced at the comment. "It's my fault, Rob. I'm sorry, man."

"I was a royal screw-up. Who wouldn't have suspected me? Let me see what I can do. I can't make any promises."

"Appreciate it," Dad said.

"Thanks, Rob." I gave Rob my cell number." I'm looking forward to meeting you."

"Don't get your hopes up."

"My fingers are crossed."

I disconnected the call.

"What just happened here?" I asked.

"What?"

"You're best buds? He's clean? You never told me."

"We aren't best buds. It started with keeping your friends close but your enemies closer mindset. He was no doubt doing the same with me. When he got clean, I saw a different person. I still had my doubts, still kept my eye on him, but became open to the possibility the murder might not involve him."

"So, all of our earlier conversations about him being a person of interest and you knew he was in on it, were just talk?"

"No. His involvement is still possible, maybe with Sabrina's arrest less probable?"

"I want to end this day on a high note. Let's not start the Sabrina thing again. Please."

"Okay."

"Thanks, Dad. I mean it. Even if he's not successful, you had my back."

"Don't make a big deal out of it."

"It's an enormous deal. I appreciate it. I'll let you know when he calls."

"You taking Vicky with you?"

"No. Persuading Maxine to allow a quick walkthrough will be easier than agreeing to a group tour."

"Agreed. Keep me posted."

Chapter 20

I watched Cooper through the window. He was jumping against a tree in the yard. A squirrel, a few feet up, looked down at him and chattered away. *That wicked squirrel is deliberately teasing my pup.* Cooper and his heckler had a two-way conversation going. Cooper was barking his head off in response to the squirrel's threats. I decided I'd better take him for a walk and wear him down before the neighbors filed a nuisance complaint.

I grabbed Cooper's leash and noticed the rose-colored glasses on the hall tree. I put them on and whistled for Cooper. I might as well kill two birds with one stone. I needed some practice with imprints before touring the Baxter place.

Portland was into human trafficking in its early days. I was bound to run into an emotional imprint walking the historic district. I needed to practice with the glasses before touring the Baxter home. Cooper came barreling through the pet door. When I leaned in to hook his leash, I saw movement out of the corner of my eye.

I stood up and pushed the glasses closer to the bridge of my nose. It was me walking to the kitchen. What? I followed. "P-Kate? That you?"

No response.

When I saw the image of me reach for the vodka bottle on top of the frig, I froze. My hands started shaking; my heart raced. I was watching a recorded image of my suicide attempt. I watched my image sit at the kitchen table, playing quarters. Just like that night, every time I missed, I took a drink and a pill. I sucked at that game. It didn't take long to finish the pills. I followed her, me, to the bedroom. I watched as she lay on the bed, her eyes drifting closed.

I took the glasses off and wiped at the tears welling up with the back of my hand. I couldn't see the vision with my naked eye. I put the glasses back on, watched the vision walk to the kitchen again and grab the vodka. It was a loop of my suicide, and I didn't have a defibrillator to shock it. I shuddered at the thought of zapping it. It seemed like such a violent thing to do to myself, even if it was an image.

Think, Katie, it's negative energy that is stuck. How do you get rid of stuck energy? Sage the place? Crystals? Vicky treated the condo with a sage smudge stick before I came home from the hospital. Smudging can't be what gets rid of the imprint or I wouldn't be seeing this now.

I took out a black tourmaline crystal from my jewelry box. Vicky gave it to me to put in my pocket when I walked through crime scenes. She said it would protect me and transform negative energy so that nothing could attach to me. By 'nothing', she meant spirits, but maybe it would work for this. I sat in front of the image and watched me take a pill. I held the crystal towards the recording.

"I'm sorry I put you through this, I'm sorry I didn't reach out for help." The image downed a few more pills. This wasn't a spirit I could interact with and talk it into going to the light, but it felt cathartic to forgive myself. Tears flowed down my cheeks with no effort on my part to bridge them back.

"I will never hurt you again. I'll fill this house with love, my heart with love." *Where did that come from? My heart? I* wasn't ready for that.

I put the crystal on the image. It passed through. I waved it back and forth through the image as it continued to play quarters. The image stood, walked to the bedroom and disappeared before reaching the bed. It worked. My hands were still shaking. There was no way I could handle any more imprints today. Cooper would have to wait for his walk. I sat back down at the table and held the crystal to my heart. *I am sorry, heart. I am.*

Chapter 21

I don't know how he pulled it off, but Rob was successful in getting Maxine to agree to a tour. I picked him up around noon. Rob filled the time with questions from his wife. She was really into psychic shows and wanted to meet me. I told him about Vicky's Psychic Development group and told him I would love to meet her and she was welcome to come and meet the group. He was jazzed. His love for his wife beamed out of him like a lighthouse bringing in ships.

It seemed like I had just picked him up and we were already at the mansion. Maxine opened the door and hugged Rob. "It's been too long. I still think this is a waste of time, but I'm happy to see you." Before he could respond, she let go of him and extended her hand. "You must be Jim's daughter, Katie?"

I shook her hand. "Yes. I appreciate your letting me do a walkthrough. As we discussed on the phone, Dad's retiring and thought being on site might generate some questions he hadn't thought of. I hope this isn't too painful."

"Can't see what good it'll do, but I won't stand in your way. I'm doing this for Rob. I'm struggling to understand the need after all these years. You have the killer in jail, but you're still investigating?"

This question was expected. The response was on the tip of my tongue when Rob jumped in.

"Thanks, sis. This is more for me than Katie. The woman they arrested may be innocent. Being falsely accused wrecks your life, and I want to help in any way possible. On some level you thought I was involved. If we can find the killer, maybe we can be close again."

Her body stiffened. "You were in London. It wasn't you."

"Then why did you turn so cold when I got back?"

Maxine looked at me and then Rob. "Let's not do this now. You have my promise we'll catch up later."

Maxine motioned for us to enter the foyer. "Ready to start the tour?"

Nodding, I donned the glasses. The room changed to a soft pink hue. Maxine's head tilted to one side, and her face took on a puzzled frown. She didn't say anything.

"Shifting the tint of what you're looking at tricks the brain. It doesn't make assumptions about what you see. The tint brings a new focus to the brain and prevents it from going into autopilot." That explanation seemed as plausible as any.

"Hmm. Interesting."

Rob added, "Makes sense to me."

"I'd like to start by imagining how the evening started. There was a wine glass in the photos. Mind if we start in the wine cellar?" My thought was it might be too emotional for Maxine if we went straight to the spot where her dad died.

"It's odd you want to start there."

"Why?"

Did she hear me? She didn't respond but continued to walk down the basement stairs. When we arrived at the bottom, she pointed to an electronic display near the door of a wooden 10x10 temperature-controlled room.

Maxine placed her thumbprint on the display and a map activated. "Dad's date that evening must have been special. This unit has the entire wine inventory and describes the location of each bottle. It also has a sensor that weighs the bottles to tell if one's been removed. It stores a date stamp and a red bottle icon next to the description to show it has been removed from the inventory."

"Fancy."

"When reviewing the inventory sometime after Dad's..." She paused. "After Dad died, I noticed the night of his... the night he died he'd opened his most cherished bottle of wine. He always talked about different scenarios that would be a reason for him to open it. The birth of a grandchild was one he always hinted at."

It didn't go unnoticed, she couldn't come out and say her dad was murdered. Rob's pained expression told me he caught the hesitation as well. "That wasn't in the notes. Did you share this with Jim?"

"Yeah. Your dad thought it was a significant clue. It's another reason he focused on finding the female on the back of the bike. That and the DNA on the robe tie."

"You're correct. The person we have in custody said he told her it was his finest wine. He was sharing it with her to toast her new life in Portland and escape from her abusive past."

"He must have really connected with her. It's surprising he opened it for someone he just met."

"She mentioned he was feeling nostalgic about your mom and the life they had. Most likely her abusive life made him feel how blessed he was to have married the love of his life."

Maxine's eyes filled with tears. "He never got over her death. The fact they were together again in heaven was the only thing that gave me solace."

Rob reached over and rested a hand on her shoulder.

She placed a hand over Rob's. "I'm okay. You don't have to do that."

He placed his hands in his pockets. "It gave me comfort too."

An awkward silence was building. Hoping to shift the mounting tension, I asked, "Is it okay if we head to the kitchen?"

"Why the kitchen?" Maxine asked.

"My guess is after he selected the wine, they went to the kitchen to pour a glass."

"Should we take a bottle with us for the full reenactment?"

"I'd love a glass," Rob said.

"That sounds great. I'd love a glass." It wasn't necessary for the investigation, but thought it might relax the two of them. Maxine didn't seem worried Rob wanted a drink. *If he was truly recovered from his addictions, wouldn't wine be off his list?*

"How about a merlot?"

"Works for me," Rob said.

"Me, too."

Maxine typed 'merlot' into the search bar of the keypad. A long list of wines and the location popped on the display. She looked over at me. "Any preference?"

"I'm clueless. You pick."

She made a selection. Although the slot number displayed next to the wine description, a green light emanated from under one of the bottles of wine to expedite finding the bottle.

"Impressive wine cellar."

"It was more than a hobby for Dad. He loved fine wine. He called his cellar the Wine Shrine."

"It is indeed a shrine."

She grabbed the bottle, and we made our way to the kitchen.

She placed it under an automatic cork remover. The cork popped in less than a second.

"Dad's favorite sound," Rob said.

Maxine laughed. The wine was a good idea. Her mood had shifted.

Wine glasses hung on a rack above the opener. Rob slid three off the frame. My eyes popped at her generous pour. I grabbed an empty glass and offered it to Maxine.

"That one is for you or Rob. I'm driving."

She nodded and poured about two ounces in my glass.

Rob took the full glass. "This one's mine."

Maxine filled the last glass higher than Rob's glass.

Rob raised an eyebrow. "I may have been too hasty in stepping up."

"There's always a second pour," Maxine offered.

"Great philosophy," he said.

Maxine took a sip, "Where to next?"

"It seems natural they would've made their way to the living room," I said.

"Follow me," she instructed.

We followed Maxine and took a seat on the larger couch.

"Like we discussed on the phone, everything changed. Not a stick of furniture remains."

"That's okay. It's more about getting a feeling. Is it okay if we sit for a moment?"

"Of course."

Rob distracted Maxine with conversation while I looked around the room. At first, nothing stood out. Shifting my position on the couch, I took a few sips of wine and completed a third-eye opening meditation Vicky taught me. My focus honed in on the spot where Maxine found her dad the night of the murder. Since the furniture was different, it was my best guess based on the proximity of the fireplace. Then, out of the corner of my eye, it happened. A vision of Maxine talking on the phone was a few feet to the right. *That must be when she called Rob. I've tapped in after the murder?* Seeing the vision made me want to do backflips, but the confusion as to why the vision started after the murder squashed the urge.

I moved my focus back to the spot on the floor. The vision shifted to James. He lay on his right ear, gazing toward Maxine's image. She looked back. His mouth moved, but his cries that night were not captured in the vision. *Was he screaming, begging for his life?* The image matched the digital photo from the crime scene. My attention turned to Rob. He and Maxine reminisced about touring wineries with their parents. They seemed so far away. My hands shook as I lowered the glass to the table.

Realizing Maxine was responsible for her father's death and Rob may have been in on it sent my heart racing. My stomach tightened, and beads of sweat pooled on my forehead. My peripheral vision caught Maxine's image again. Her imprint moved to the fireplace. She opened the painting like a door. Moving the painting revealed an embedded safe. The vision placed her index finger on a display next to the safe. The image shifted to Maxine holding a gun and walking toward James. *Cutting off his finger was meant to throw off the police. She didn't need it to open the safe. She had access.*

She called Rob before murdering her dad! Was he in on it? He had to have heard James screaming in the background. Could I trust him? I wish I had taken the driverless vehicle. A second pour sounded good. How would the ride back play out?

"Hey Rob, did you know your dad was alive when Maxine called you?"

Fingers snapped in front of me. The vision disappeared. "Are you okay? You broke out in a sweat and are pale as a ghost." Rob placed his hand on my shoulder. It was gentle, but it still made me uncomfortable.

"I'm, I'm, it's the wine. Red wine triggers hot flashes. I got a bit dizzy. It's passed. I'm good."

"Do you need anything to eat? Will that help?" Maxine looked worried as she stood next to Rob.

"Please, don't fuss. I'm good." The two of them hovering over me made me want to reach for my gun. Fortunately, it was locked in the glove box.

"Do you need me to drive us back?"

"No, I'm good. Speaking of driving, we should get going. We've imposed long enough."

Maxine didn't object. "Let me walk you out."

Chapter 22

We said our goodbyes. Rob promised Maxine he would come for dinner on Sunday. Somehow, I managed a smile and thanked her for her time.

My mind spun when I started the car. I couldn't get an arrest warrant based on the imprint of the murder. It would take physical evidence.

Rob broke me out of my thoughts.

"Did you see anything?"

"What?"

"Did you see or feel anything that confirms Sabrina's innocence? Did you see her with Dad?"

"No." That was honest. I didn't see her with James. I had to gauge if he was in on it or what he knew about that night.

"That's a shame."

I could hear Dad's word's playing back in my head when I asked if Rob might have hired someone to kill James. *More on the realm of probable.* Why would he say that when he and Rob had gotten close over the years? If he believed it, why was he so hard-headed about Sabrina? We had no evidence that they knew each other.

Rob stared down at his hands. The smile he wore all afternoon was gone. P-Kate's words echoed in my head. *Blood is thicker than water.* Blood is thicker than water, which means there was no way I could break a family tie. Based on that, sharing my vision could backfire. He could run straight to Maxine and tell her everything. I thought about the second riddle. In her usual fashion, P-Kate gave opposing messages one after the other. It was on me to pick which one resonated. *The ties that bind are the hardest to break, but that doesn't mean you can't stretch them to the limit.* Okay, that meant Rob could be trusted with the truth. *Stretch them to the limit? Maybe not all the truth?* Was P-Kate's third message a tie-breaker? *Just know that people can change. A second chance is worth a second look.* Turns out that hint wasn't about Sabrina being the girl next door turned killer. Was

Rob's rehab successful? Had he changed? He drank wine tonight and seemed interested in getting the fullest glass. He could have been joking, or maybe he needed wine.

"Rob?"

"Yes?"

"Tell me to mind my business if this is too personal. I noticed you had wine tonight. My dad mentioned your rehab was successful, and you turned things around after your dad died. You hinted at a strained relationship with your sister. Did I cause you to drink by putting you two together again?"

"What? No. We both work for the company. Sure, we rarely see each other, but it's not because we can't stand each other. The stress of Dad's murder pulled us apart. We didn't draw strength from each other, but we didn't become enemies either."

"You said you thought she blamed you."

"I don't think she thought I wanted him dead, but she probably wondered if I had someone break in to steal the cash from the safe. Only the family knew about the safe and that his fingerprint activated it. Being in London, I wouldn't be a suspect."

"Was she able to access the safe with her fingerprint?"

"Yes, Dad trusted her and gave her full access to the accounts and the safe. Why?"

"That seems to rule her out since she could open the safe if she wanted to. Were you aware of the gun in the safe?"

"No. He never opened the safe in front of me. If I happened to walk in on him, he would close it the second I entered the room. That used to irritate the shit out of me. Acting like I was going to snap, push him aside, and start grabbing money." He shook his head at the memory.

I tried to plant a seed with my 'rule-her-out' comment. It might be too risky to follow with, 'unless she was trying to make it look like a robbery.'

"So, if I didn't cause you to drink tonight, does that mean you aren't clean?"

"I'm no longer addicted to drugs or alcohol. I still drink but can stop. Zero desire to continue drinking after one or even two glasses of alcohol and haven't touched a drug since the program."

"Don't alcoholics have to abstain?"

"It seems odd to cure addiction with a drug, but the program was unique. We used peyote in our group therapy sessions. It's a psychedelic, mind-bending drug that causes spiritual visions. When users connect with the universe and the creator, it changes the brain forever. The ego dissolves away, and materialism is no longer a driver of behavior. There is only one consuming desire: stay connected to source."

"Sounds powerful."

"Life changing. It's helped so many addicts come clean. I'm a social drinker, but have no desire for drugs or alcohol."

I stretched the tie to the limit. "I'm disappointed I didn't see the murder. Wait. That sounds horrible. I don't want to see your dad killed. You know what I mean."

"Yeah, I get it."

"There was something significant, though."

"Yeah?"

"Maxine was talking to someone on the phone. I'm guessing it was when she called you about the murder. The powerful emotion of finding him caused the imprint. Maybe he was still knocked out before his murder so it didn't record?"

"Maybe."

"Can you tell me about your conversation with Maxine that night?"

"I played it back in my head for so many years, but it has faded. She was so upset she couldn't get the words out. After she calmed down, she told me what happened and that it was fate. I was lucky it happened before he changed the will. I'd still get my inheritance. I remember telling her it wasn't fate. The program was working. I tried to tell her about my spiritual experiences, but she said I was delusional and was trading one drug for another. Staying clean was impossible, and we both knew it."

"Did you hear anything in the background?"

"Like what?"

"Any strange sounds? Voices?"

He was silent for a moment and closed his eyes as if to dive deep into his memory bank. "The TV was on? Yeah, the TV was definitely on. She kept yelling at the virtual assistant to turn it down but it didn't. It must've been offline."

"What kind of sound?"

"I couldn't make anything out but, I was so focused on the news, it was like I was in a deep tunnel."

My gut told me he wasn't in on it. *Could he handle the news? Was I jumping the gun, discussing my visions with him before getting with the team?*

"Rob?"

"Yes."

"Rob, this may be hard to hear. Do you think it could've been your dad in the background?" I left out he was alive in the vision. Stretch it to the limit.

"That would mean... No. No way. Maxine had unlimited access to her inheritance; she didn't need the money. She worried about me but wouldn't kill him for me. I'm not the reason he's dead!"

"Rob..."

"No. Stop!" He hit the dashboard. "That's not how it happened."

"Would you at least consider the possibility?"

He stared out the window as I pulled out of the circular driveway.

I needed to run this by Vicky. Rob wouldn't turn on his sister. I've no doubt she killed James, but Rob wasn't there yet. If he got there, he still wouldn't turn on his sister. Blood is thicker than water.

Chapter 23

After dropping Rob off, I asked Vicky to meet me at Papa Fu's. She was about 10 minutes away. With the food order out of the way, I sipped hot tea until she got there.

I saw Vicky at the entrance and waved to catch her attention. She took her coat off and plopped down so hard the booth shook. "Did you order the spicy shrimp for me?"

"Of course." I raised two glasses of water. "The waitress brought some water. I held off ordering a drink because I wasn't sure if you wanted tea or something stronger."

"It's like you know me." She laughed. "You sounded tense on the phone. Are we going deep or having a fun girls' night?"

"It'll make the Grand Canyon look like a crack in the sidewalk."

"That deep. Jeez, I'd better keep my wits about me. She pointed to one of the glasses. "That'll do."

I handed her the glass and set mine down. "I was right about Sabrina. She didn't kill James."

"Outstanding. What's the bad news?"

"It was his daughter, Maxine."

"That explains why James doesn't want his murder solved. You've got to make him understand about their contractual agreement. The act of murdering her father may have settled the karmic debt. But, if she wants to grow from the experience, she must atone. She has to go to jail. It's the only way."

"What if he doesn't care? What then?"

I looked up at the waitress holding out one plate in front of her. "Who had the basil fried rice and chicken?"

I raised my hand.

"You must be spicy shrimp." She placed the plate in front of Vicky.

"Who're you calling a shrimp?" Vicky laughed.

The waitress chuckled. "You're hilarious. Can I get you anything else?"

I shook my head.

"Looks like we're all set," Vicky responded.

"I'll check on you in a bit. Enjoy."

Vicky took a bite, sat back, and rolled her eyes. "This is even more delicious than last time. Want a bite?"

"No. I've got enough for a family of four on my plate." I took a few bites waiting for her to continue. She kept eating like it was her first meal in days.

"Um, James. What if he doesn't care about the contractual agreement?"

She sipped her water. "Right. Sorry. Skipped breakfast and lunch. It's been a crazy day. Remember when we first talked about life contracts a few weeks ago? About how we make these agreements before we are born?"

I nodded. "These tend to be family members that stick together across lifetimes, taking turns being parent, spouse, child, or even close friends or business partners," I said.

"Good job. You were listening and get an A+. In the spirit of going deeper tonight, I'll school you some more. At each passing, you join your guide for a debriefing on the lessons you learned and the experiences you gained. These are reviewed against any life contracts or agreements made before you incarnated. Agreements are not always fulfilled. Each person in the contract has free will and can alter or sever the agreement once incarnated."

"What happens if you break the contract?"

"During the review, if it is determined there are parts of the contract you didn't honor or complete or, worse, you behaved in such a way you incurred additional karmic debt, you move to the next phase which is the intake phase. In this area, you regroup with your core members and an elder to facilitate the group discussion. You and your core group will make new agreements for experiences in the next life to help course correct and bring everyone further along the spiritual path. As a group, you can also decide to stay and dissolve the outstanding contractual terms, but that will mean you won't raise your spiritual vibration. If everyone in the group chooses to continue the lessons, the contract is amended with the new terms for the next incarnation."

"So earth is basically a place where you play out spiritual growth opportunities?"

Vicky touched the tip of her finger to her nose. "Exactly. When you're born into a human body, you're a spiritual being having a human experience. Earth is one gigantic spiritual rehab center. The opportunities can include resolving karmic debts, self-healing, raising others vibrations, or having experiences that promote your personal spiritual growth."

"So we need to tell Maxine to honor her agreement with James and turn herself in. Why didn't you tell me that earlier?"

"That's the glitch in the process. To fully grow, you can't have a memory of your agreements when you're born. It has to unfold organically as you live out your life. Once a soul inhabits the human body, all memory is wiped from the consciousness."

"No one on earth has a conscious memory of any agreements with their core group?"

Vicky didn't answer. She took a pen from her purse, grabbed a napkin, and drew an octopus with way more than eight tentacles. Some tentacles were short, some medium, most were long.

"Is the spicy shrimp channeling a message from an octopus?"

"You wanted to go deep. Stop me if this becomes too much."

"I want to understand. What's with the gazillionpus?"

Vicky drew a line separating the head from the mantel and tentacles. She wrote the words 'spiritual realm higher self' at the head, 'souls' at the mantel, and 'unfoldment' at the squiggly lines representing the tentacles. She tapped the pen on the head. "Think of the head as representing the higher self. The mantel, instead of housing the organs, holds the divine oversoul. The higher self doesn't incarnate. It's never born into a human body. It remains in the spiritual realm directly connected to source, God, Universal Energy. It's called many things, depending on the belief structure."

"And the Oversoul?"

"It holds the cumulative life experiences and is the level between the soul and the higher self. It's the universal spirit that lives in all souls. At the higher self, all the fragments are assembled into one higher consciousness holding the infinite possibilities for each soul's journey. I guess you could say it is a program that holds the energetic code of the soul's journey across all lifetimes. The tentacles represent the path to and from heaven for each soul. It's what some describe as a tunnel when they cross over."

"Okay."

"You asked me if anyone on earth has a conscious memory of their agreements. This is a visual for you. There is no conscious memory. That's why very few people complete their contract and they keep having to repeat the lesson. It's a slow process lasting over several lifetimes."

"Sounds like we are doing things the hard way."

"That's the design, to awaken to our soul's purpose, behave in a way that honors that purpose, and reconnect with God or Source. There are hints and nudges sent from the higher self in the forms of dreams and insights." She drew a line from the head down a few tentacles and drew several circles representing the suction holes along the tentacle. She tapped the pen on a circle. "Once in the human body, the direct connection gets a bit muddled if the incarnated soul is in their head all the time or is focused on what they don't want, that blocks the message. If they mediate, eat cleanly, and work on their spiritual connection, the insights get through as dreams or intuition. The more the person listens, the more messages are received."

She drew a circle around a tentacle. "Each tentacle or arm represents a parallel soul's journey. Each soul is encoded with the energetic code of that soul's journey over several lifetimes to include all agreements. It is encoded in the DNA and can be accessed by the subconscious and superconscious. The superconscious holds the real identity and has a direct link to the higher self. It is the connection of Source within you. Think of each sucker on the arm as a past life, present life, or future life."

"Is that why some of the arms in your drawing are different sizes?"

"Yes, the longer arm represents someone who has incarnated over several lifetimes. The shorter ones represent young souls." She put a star in one of the arms.

"The arms to the right or left hold parallel lives closest to this soul's life. She drew a line up the arm and to the head, the higher self. "When you crossed over, your desire to see your mom and Jim again pulled you into the closest tentacle holding that life. Instead of returning to your physical body, you floated around P-Kate's world." She circled a sucker in the next tentacle.

"How did I get back in my, um, tentacle?"

"I think our love for you and prayers for your recovery pulled you back into your physical body."

"Thank you."

"It wasn't me; it was all of us. God, your friends, family, guides. It was a team effort."

"Is there another way to remember without crossing over?"

"Some cultures use mind-altering drugs."

"Rob told me he took peyote and had a life-changing spiritual experience."

"He opened his superconsciousness and connected with his higher self. I doubt Maxine remembers her contract, but Rob may remember the core agreement. He may be willing to help us."

"If Maxine doesn't remember the contract and Rob helps us, she will think he turned on her. Won't that set up a karmic obligation if he turns on her?"

"Not if it's part of the core agreement. We can look into that if Rob is willing."

Blood's thicker than water. "Uh, maybe we hold off on pulling Rob in. What's another way to remember the agreement?"

"People go to someone like me. Someone that can read the Akashic records."

"I don't think she is open to psychic stuff."

"It's not just if she's open to it. Her guides have to allow the records to be read. I can't just tell what I see unless the person's guide agrees. They may not be ready to hear it, and it can cause downstream issues such as seeking revenge versus trying to heal."

"Will my guides let you tell me about my contract with Dad?"

"Yes."

"Well?"

"I'll tell you the main lesson you agreed to learn in this lifetime is resolving abandonment issues."

"That's a failed lesson. I feel like Dad abandoned me when Mom and Jimmy died. What else do you have for me?"

"That's all I can share, hon."

"I guess I'll see Dad again in the next life then."

Vicky smiled. "The good news is after crossing over, James is in a place now where he remembers making the agreement with his daughter and why. It's not only to fulfill a karmic debt. That's one part. The agreement is also so she can ascend dimensions quicker. By agreeing to suffer the consequences of killing him, she can skip several incarnations. Who knows, she may even be able to stop incarnating and stay in heaven. James understands the unconditional love parents have for their children. He'll listen."

"It strikes me as odd that parents support their kids even if they're killers."

"It's an eternal bond. It may satisfy him that she completed their contract, but you need to tap into his unconditional love for her and explain he's hurting her spiritual growth. She could have another dark experience in the next lifetime. He can help her raise her spiritual vibration by helping you solve the case."

"Why is that important?"

"Before she returned to earth, Maxine made a conscious decision to end the karmic debt between them. She could kill him and be even for whatever transgression he did to her in a past lifetime. Maxine wanted to experience the dark night of the soul to have a spiritual awakening. Murdering him might clear up their debt, but atoning will increase her vibration and move her closer to enlightenment. If she doesn't suffer the consequences of her actions, she won't grow spiritually as she intended."

"How do you know that's her goal? Maybe she wanted to call it even and live out her life. It's not a terrible life. She's worth billions."

"It's what I'm getting from the Akashic records. James can share their agreement with you. I doubt she didn't want to raise her vibration as part of the agreement. Material possessions don't have the appeal that connecting to God does when you're on the other side when you're thinking clearly, and designing your agreements before incarnating. Don't get me wrong; being poor doesn't make you spiritual. You can be wealthy and spiritual. Nothing wrong with wanting wealth, a better life, or even desiring things. It's how you stay aligned and connected that keeps you on the spiritual path, not what you gain or abstain from."

"I guess even if he doesn't want to help, having him acknowledge and remember their agreement may keep him from getting upset. I'd rather not have my condo turned into a wind tunnel again if we make an arrest."

"Sounds like you're okay with crossing over."

"Not thrilled with the thought, but I'll do it. I'm just not sure how. Juliet connected me to Sarah when I crossed over last time. How can I find James once I'm on the other side? I'm not going to ask for Juliet's help after she hijacked my body."

"Ask Rob to give you something that belonged to James. You can hold it during your third-eye meditation. Think of him, and you will be pulled to him."

"What if I don't trade souls? Will the connection to James be as strong if I astral project? I'm not ready for a repeat of being blocked from my body."

"This is the last thing you want to hear, but you're going to need to cross over. Astral projection will only put you in observer mode. It's a lower vibration, and you won't be able to interact with James or discuss life contracts at that level."

"Can someone else on the team do it?"

"They can, but what's the likelihood James will listen to them? You're connected to this case. It needs to be you."

"Who will I trade souls with?"

"I've been thinking about that. Do you know anyone that has crossed over you'd trust with your life?"

"Silly question. Jimmy, Mom, and Grams."

"Just wanted you to know it and feel it. Which of the three would benefit from trading places?"

"Mom could see Dad again. Dad never got to say goodbye. He could have closure. I think he would be open to it."

"Talk to your dad tonight, get something personal that belonged to James, and we'll get everything set up at the office."

"Hey, do you mind if I invite Rob's wife to the session? She wants to develop her skills. She can bring the object with her."

"I don't mind at all. Would Rob want to join?"

"I'll make the offer, but I don't think he's ready to entertain the thought that Maxine murdered their dad. Let's leave it as an exercise to see if James can give us details around his murder. We won't discuss the details until after they leave the office."

"I'll let the team know to hold back on any discussions about Maxine."

"Schools out. I'm not a fan of cold Spicy Shrimp, and I'm still starving."

"Well then, dig in." I picked up my napkin and placed it on my lap "Thanks for this."

Vicky nodded as she chewed on a forkful of her dinner.

Chapter 24

The meeting was arranged. Dad was excited about seeing mom again. To my surprise, he admitted seeing me connect with Rose's Oma, and their emotional exchange made him wonder what he would say to her if she were able to come through. He said he'd been talking to her and asking her for forgiveness for years. To hear her acknowledge his regrets and forgive him for not being there would mean everything to him.

I knew it would be a healing moment for them both. Part of me wished I could witness their reunion, but I needed to connect with James.

Rob and his wife Sharon jumped on the chance to join the session. Rob said he would bring his dad's favorite watch.

I was setting up chairs in a circle when the three of them walked into the room.

"Did you guys drive here together?"

"No. We decided to meet for lunch," Rob said, handing me his dad's watch. "I'm getting that back, right?"

"Of course."

Rob's wife held her hand out eagerly. "I'm Rob's wife Sharon. Thank you for letting me join the session. I've been dying to meet you ever since Rob mentioned a psychic was working on his dad's case."

I was a bit startled. She could pass for Vicky's twin. I shook her hand and introduced her to the team. "You're about to go from zero to sixty in a few moments. What you're going to see isn't the kind of channeling you see on your psychic TV shows. I'm going to leave my body and let my mom step in so she and Dad can have closure. While Mom and Dad are catching up, I'm going to see if James will tell us who killed him." I felt bad about not having full transparency. I looked at Vicky for moral support.

She smiled. "Let's get started. Everyone, take a seat."

Just like with Sarah, there was one seat empty for Mom to agree to transfer and to return when I was ready to come back. She had to agree before I could let her in my body. Earlier I had shared with Vicky that this step seemed unnecessary. It was Mom. She wasn't going to block me from returning. She agreed but held fast with the position the process was there for a reason. She wasn't comfortable skipping steps.

"Katie, reach your mom using the third-eye meditation and let her know what we are trying to do."

"I did that this morning. She loved the idea."

"Perfect. Close your eyes and connect with her. Let her know we are ready."

"Um, before we swap, Rob, is there anything you want me to share with your dad?"

"Can you tell Dad I love him and I'm sorry for all the pain, aggravation, and anguish I caused him?"

"I'm certain he knows but, yes, I'll tell him. I'm sure your mom will be with him. Any messages for her?"

"I love her and I miss her. I'm sorry she suffered so much from the cancer. She was the best mother I could ask for, and I wish we had more time together."

Tears welled in my eyes and a lump formed in my throat. I felt the same way about my Mom. She didn't suffer from cancer, but the death of my brother ate at her like metastatic cancer. I wish I'd been able to help her heal from his death.

Sharon added a request. "Can you tell them hi for me? I'm sorry I never met them, but I'm taking good care of their son. I love him with all my heart. They raised a great guy and would be proud of him."

"Will do."

Rob blushed and leaned into her. "Aw, love you, too, Princess."

Their exchange defused some of my nervousness.

I closed my eyes and called out to Mom in my mind. *"We're ready for you. Can you sit beside me before trading souls? It's protocol. I forgot to mention it this morning. Vicky needs to know that you understand the swap is temporary and that you have to return."*

I didn't hear a response in my mind, but Vicky acknowledged Mom was in the room. I couldn't see her but heard her tell Vicky she knew the exchange was temporary.

"What do I do now?" she asked.

How I missed that voice. I could tell that Dad couldn't hear her or see her since she wasn't in body. He kept looking at Vicky, me, and the empty chair, confused. Rob and Sharon had their eyes glued to where Mom would be sitting.

"We need you to walk toward Katie and sit on her lap. You will slide into her body. Sitting this way makes the process gentler for your daughter. Please begin."

Vicky could see Mom, so she knew that Mom had entered my body. She clued everyone in when she said, "Good job, Mrs. Hanson."

I could feel Mom and hear her in my mind. It was like being wrapped in love and joy. *"Mom, I miss you so much. I wish I could hug you."*

I felt her laugh. "Hug, schmug, we can't get much closer than this. I love you, too, baby girl."

"I've got to leave my body now. Sorry about the audience, I wasn't thinking about the two of you needing privacy. I can ask everyone to step out of the room."

"Nonsense, who couldn't benefit from hearing two people express their love for each other."

"Then it's time," I said in my mind." Out loud, I said, "I'm ready."

"Katie, you know this part. Close your eyes and focus your attention on your third eye. Hold the watch tight and picture James. Do you have him in your mind's eye?"

"Yes."

"Now put your attention on the center of your forehead. Take slow deep breaths until you see that soft swirl of the tunnel you entered before. Can you see it?"

"Yes."

"Like before, focus on the swirl and mentally picture yourself leaping out of your chair and into the tunnel. Can you imagine this?"

I nodded my head.

"Keep picturing it," she said.

I heard a sound similar to a cork popping and felt a pulling sensation out of my body. I didn't see the tunnel but was aware I was out of my body.

I looked around. James wasn't here. *The watch didn't pull me to him.* I sent a mental message. *James, please, talk to me. I have a message from your son.*

James appeared in front of me. His wife was next to him. He didn't say anything. She nudged him. "Don't be rude, hon. Listen to what the nice lady has to say. Pleased to meet you, dear." Her smile was toothy but not in a creepy way. It was comforting.

James spoke in a soft, gentle voice. "What's the message? Is he okay?"

I hadn't expected kindness or concern knowing their contentious relationship.

"He's good, great, actually. I told him I wanted to talk to you about Maxine, and he asked if I could give you a message."

He started to step back at the mention of Maxine. His wife held his arm fast, to keep him in place.

"He wants you both to know how much he loves and misses you. He's sorry for all the grief he caused you both."

James spoke first. "You tell my boy." He paused and looked at his wife. She stroked his arm, prompting him to continue.

"You tell my son I love him, and I'm the one who should be ashamed, not him. I pushed my will on him. I didn't help him become the man he was meant to be. Instead I forced him to become a version of me. Never considering what he wanted. Never allowing him to grow into the amazing man he is now. Had I not passed, I think he'd still be an addict.

He wouldn't have found that lovely lady. He wouldn't have known the same kind of love his mom and I have. I'm the schmuck in this scenario, not Rob. He has nothing to apologize for."

I listened intently as he bore his soul about the love he had for Rob, his regrets, and desire for Rob to follow his passion. He knew his son's heart wasn't in the business, despite the incredible job he was doing.

"I'll let him know. I know he'll appreciate hearing this. I'm just getting to know your son and can tell he wants nothing more than to please both of you."

"I know now it's not his job to please us. It's his job to figure out his passion and follow his dreams. That's it. Nothing would please us more."

Rob's mom nodded.

"I'll let him know. Can we talk about Maxine? I know you want to protect her, but I want to explain that you may be hurting her spiritual growth by letting her get away with your murder."

"When I crossed over, all of our agreements over all our lifetimes became clear. Before I incarnated back to earth, I agreed to be murdered as part of my soul contract with Maxine. I don't want to share the horrible things I've done to her soul over several life times. I can say a bullet to the head was letting me off easy."

"Was part of her agreement to serve time in prison?"

"It was, but it's not necessary. I'm where I want to be." He kissed his wife's hand. "It all worked out. She killed me like we agreed, and I'm back in the arms of the love of my life. It's all settled."

"Except it's not," I said.

"Hon, you know she's right. We learned that in our recovery group."

I needed to play the unconditional love card. "You were the best father to her. Your love for her is unconditional, and you want the best for her. You always have."

They both nodded.

"Because of that, we need to arrest her. She needs to complete the contract by honoring the second part. She needs to serve time in prison."

"I'm sorry. I don't know if I can help."

"I don't need you to do anything. Well, that is unless you know what she did with the gun. Do you?"

"No. I crossed immediately. The room filled with an amazing bright light and then I saw this beautiful lady holding out her hand." He kissed his wife on the top of her head. She was shoulder level and it seemed like it was something he did every chance he got.

"I can't help. Sorry."

"I guess all I can ask is you're okay with it. That you won't interfere or hurt me or anyone that tries to arrest your daughter."

"Sorry about your office. I didn't even know I could do that."

"It's okay. Just don't do it again." I laughed.

He squeezed his wife's hand. "You have my word."

"Thank you both. It may feel like you're causing her pain but, in the end, you'll be helping her end the karmic debt between the two of you. I have no doubt when she fulfills your agreement, your next incarnation together will be in a loving, supportive, joyous family for all of you. No trauma or drama to speak of."

"That sounds lovely, dear."

I looked Maxine's mom in the eye. "Are you okay with her going to prison?"

"It breaks my heart, but I understand."

"This one's way ahead of me on the path. I'm surprised they let me hang with her. I'm definitely not in her league," James said.

She hugged him. "You just joined my league."

He hugged her back. It was a long hug. I didn't think he would ever let her go.

"Thanks for talking to me. I'm going to leave you guys now and spend some time with my brother before I head back."

"Don't forget to tell Rob what we talked about," he said.

"I won't."

I thought of my brother and visualized the small silver cord that connected us and would draw me to him.

"Hey, sis. Good to see you again."

I opened my eyes. I was standing in front of Jimmy and gave him a big hug.

"It's great what you did for Mom and Dad. I've been watching. It's beautiful to see them forgive each other."

"You've been watching? Can I see?"

"You're only here temporarily, so you haven't been given the ability to check in. I'll catch you up to what I've seen so far."

Chapter 25

"How are you feeling Mrs. Hanson?" Vicky asked.

"I feel like I just stepped off a roller coaster going 200 miles an hour."

"Put your pinky and thumb together. It grounds you."

Vicky grabbed a piece of candy from the dish on the conference table.

"Put this in your mouth, the sugar will help."

"It's Frances. Call me Frances, not Mrs. Hanson. Mrs. makes me sound like a school teacher." She popped the piece in her mouth.

"I see where Katie gets her humor."

"Certainly not from me," Jim spoke as he knelt in front of Katie's body.

Frances reached for his hands and pulled him up. She gave him a hug.

"How are you doing, you old coot?"

"I'm a lost soul without you."

"You were always the poet." She stroked his hair.

"Can you ever forgive me for leaving you and Katie?"

"I know why you did it. I get it. Can you forgive me for not seeing the signs, for shutting down and not being there for you?" he said.

"I told you the night you wrote the letter there was nothing to forgive. You must not have heard me. I needed to be with our son. I couldn't stand the thought of him being alone. It was so overwhelming. I couldn't think of anything else. Not even how it would hurt you and my sweet Katie. I'm so sorry."

"You were with me when I wrote the letter? I thought I smelled your perfume. I told myself it was you, but then my practical side told me it was lingering on the curtains and bedding."

"The letter is still in your wallet, right?"

"Uh, yes."

Katie's dad opened his wallet and retrieved a worn piece of notebook paper.

"Go ahead and read it. I'm listening," Frances said.

He looked around the room and cleared his throat. His voice shook as he read.

It's been a week now. I'm still so mad I could scream and tear apart this house with my bare hands. I wonder if I'm mad at you for taking the pills or me for not seeing the signs. If I had paid closer attention, could I have done something to give you the will to live? I'm positive I'll never muster the strength to live without you. I can appreciate the pull you must have felt to take your life and be with our son again. I feel that same pull to join you both. For Katie's sake, I'll resist. I ask God for the strength to stay each and every day.

When I came home after the service, I could smell your perfume lingering in the air. I felt you near me. For a moment, I imagined we would grow old together. I stood in your closet and breathed you in.

I broke down at the thought of the fragrance fading like a distant memory. I grabbed your perfume bottle and placed it in my nightstand. I vowed once a week I would spray the pillowcase next to me.

When I closed my eyes that night, I saw you, felt you pressed against me. I strained to hear your snore. The snore that kept me up counting sheep for years. The snore I would give my right arm to hear again.

I'm filled with regret. Regret for putting work first, for not showing you how much I loved you each day. Regret for pushing you away after Jimmy died. Embarrassed because I wasn't there for you to lean on, to turn to. Would you have stayed had I not shut down?

It's probably the perfume messing with my senses, but I know you're with me, I know that I'm not growing old alone and find comfort in that.

I know you're watching me so I stopped leaving my dirty clothes on the floor. I place them in the hamper just like you always wanted. A few times I threw them on the floor hoping to hear you nag at me as you gathered each piece. But all I heard was an unbearable deafening silence.

I had a dream last night that you were with Jimmy again. The two of you were laughing and hugging. I longed to hold you both, but the dream ended before I reached you. I woke up and knew you were where you needed to be. I can't recall you smiling since his death and had forgotten how beautiful it was. My heart is still heavy with a weight that will never be lifted, but knowing our son is with you makes it a little easier to breathe. I forgive you and will always love you.

"Thank you for forgiving me and writing that beautiful note," she said.

He set the paper on the table, grabbed a tissue, and blew his nose. It was so loud it sounded like a flock of geese.

Both Rob and Sharon pulled tissue from the box and dabbed at their eyes as they laughed at the sound that vibrated around the room.

"My snore is no match for that bull-horn at the end of your face."

Jim gave another blow. Mostly for laughs.

Frances turned serious. She stepped back. "Katie is here. I need to go."

Everyone stood still and stared at her.

"What happens now?" Jim asked.

"Mrs. Hanson, I mean Frances. Please take a seat," Vicky instructed.

She gave Jim another hug before returning to her chair.

He sat in the empty chair next to her and held her hand.

"Frances, you're going to leave the same way Katie did."

"Focus on the center of your forehead."

****

"Wait, Mom, don't go yet," I screamed in my head.

Fully back in my body, I held up my hand to let Vicky know we needed more time.

"What is it, baby girl?"

"I love you. I wish you could stay."

"I love you, too. You know how to reach me. You call out to me anytime you need me. Both Jimmy and I are with you always."

"I know. It's not the same. I need you."

"You have me, angel; you know that. Did you get what you needed from your visit?"

"Not really, but I think it was a good visit for James and will be healing for Rob. His dad's proud of him, and I know he needed to hear that."

"We're all proud of you, too. You know that right?"

"Yes. It's nice to hear, though."

"I've got to go, hon. Good luck with your case. We'll be watching and will help in any way we can."

"Bye, Mom."

"She's gone," I said, looking around the room. There wasn't a dry eye in the house. "What happened here?"

"It was a bit of a bawl fest," Rob admitted.

"Grab some more tissue. It's not over."

Everyone, including me, grabbed a tissue and took our seats.

"I shared your message with your dad. He wants you to know that you have nothing to apologize for. It's your dad who wants to apologize."

"To me? What did he do to me other than try and fix me?"

"It wasn't his role to fix you. He thinks he's the one that broke you. He regrets not showing you the same unconditional love he showed Maxine. He treated you differently and, because of that, he failed as a father."

"He didn't fail me. He gave me everything, every opportunity, more chances to change than he should've," Rob said.

"As a parent, his role was to help influence and guide you, not to manipulate and force you into meeting his expectations of what your life should be like. He told me to tell you your life's contract isn't to be the person he wanted you to be. It is to find your joy and passion. He said to tell you how proud he is of you for turning your life around. For finding a love as amazing as the love he had for your mom."

Rob leaned over and kissed Sharon on the head. *Like father, like son.* I was certain it was something he'd seen James do a thousand times.

"He wanted me to tell you how proud he is that you're working in the business. You're doing an amazing job. That being said, he wanted me to tell you to quit. The business was his life, not yours. He is releasing you to follow your passion. He wants you to know that he recognizes it isn't where you want to be. You're honoring his dream of you running the business."

Rob's body wracked with sobs. Sharon held him tight and rocked him against her chest, like a small child. The sobs subsided. He straightened and walked over to me with such speed I didn't have time to register before he was in front of me, lifting me off the ground in a bear hug. "I can't tell you what this means to me."

"Or me." Dad joined in for a group hug.

"Or me." Sharon wrapped her arms around us.

"I'm feeling the love here." Vicky leaned in and put one arm around Rob and the other around Sharon.

Rob broke from the group. "How about you? Did Dad tell you who killed him?"

"He said he couldn't help. I got pieces that I'm not sure how to put together. I need to talk to the team to sort things out. Is it okay if I reach out to you later?"

"Yes. Do you need us to head out?"

"Do you need to talk? I just laid a lot on you."

"Are you kidding? I feel like floating out of the room. I've been given a new lease on life—Dad's right. The job is sucking the life out of me. I hate it. Always have."

"I remember your saying that on our first call together. I thought it was an expression that you were working too hard. So what do you want to be when you grow up?"

"A writer." He punched Jim on the arm. "Not sure I'll be as good as this old coot."

"What do you mean?"

He pointed to the piece of paper on the conference table. "Your dad wrote a real tear-jerker letter to your mom."

I walked over to the table and picked it up. "Can I read it?"

"You can have it. Turns out your mom was with me when I wrote it, and I just read it to her. It's not something I need to carry anymore."

I held it to my chest, not sure if I was ready to read it. Rob and Sharon gave me one last hug.

"I'll call you later," he said.

I handed him the watch. "Sounds good. You two get home safe."

He tucked it in his pocket and gave me another hug. "This watch means even more now."

Sharon took her arm in his and walked him out.

Dad started stacking the chairs. I leaned against the table, grabbed another tissue, and read the note. The words leapt off the page:

> I can appreciate the pull you must
> have felt to take your life and be with
> our son Jim again. I feel that same pull
> to join you both. For the sake of Katie,
> I'll resist. I ask God for strength to stay
> each and every day.

Our contract is complete. Dad didn't abandon me in this lifetime. He found the strength to stay because of me. I watched him through tear-stained eyes as he finished stacking chairs. He caught me looking at him and stopped. "You okay?"

I ran over and hugged him. "I love you, Dad."

He hugged me back. "Me, too, baby girl."

I dropped the letter when I hugged him. Mom's cross necklace slipped out of my shirt and hung in the air when I bent down for the letter.

"You're wearing your mom's necklace."

I held it in my hand and stood up. "I never take it off... Wait, Dad, that's it! I never take it off!"

"That's nice. You always wear it."

"No, I mean, I never take it off! It makes me feel close to Mom. It holds her essence. Remember, Maxine said the same thing."

"What are you talking about?"

"When you filled me in on the case, you said you weren't sure what upset Maxine more, her dad being murdered or losing her mom's jewelry."

"Okay."

"Remember, I said I hoped it was losing her dad."

"I don't remember exactly."

"You said it wasn't that she didn't love James. Her mom died when she was young, and the jewelry was all that she had and... 'it held her mom's essence!'"

"Okay. You feel the same way."

Oh crap. I just realized Dad doesn't know Maxine killed James. No wonder this wasn't making sense. "Dad, Rob doesn't know this yet but, when he took me to the Baxter home, I saw an image of Maxine killing James."

"Maxine killed James?"

"She came in and found James tied up and killed him. Her fingerprint opened the safe. She cut off his finger to make it look like a robbery. When she called Rob, I could see James screaming and trying to untie himself."

"Did she shoot him with Rob on the phone? Were they in on it together? I just hugged the son of a ... "

"No. She shot him after she hung up. I couldn't hear the conversation, but I'm certain he has no idea she shot James. Well, until I shared part of the vision. I asked him to think about the possibility. Maxine made it look like a robbery but, if she feels even half of the connection with her mom's jewelry as I do, she'd never get rid of it. She may have ditched the gun, but no way would she have gotten rid of something so personal from her mom. We prove she has them and maybe we can get a warrant to search for the gun."

"We can't get a warrant to search for a bunch of necklaces and rings. There's nothing that we could say to convince a judge."

"I didn't say we needed to find the pieces. We only need to prove that she still has them."

"What do you mean?"

"Remember when I found Sabrina, I said I used a special program and couldn't share the details?"

"Yes."

"You have to keep this a secret. It's an object recognition program. I can ask Nick's friend Paul to run Maxine's photo through the program to see if we can find images of her wearing the jewelry after the murder. We have photos that were given to the insurance company and their inventory sheet in the case files. If Paul agrees, I'll send them to him and we can go from there."

Dad didn't seem as excited as I was.

"What's wrong?"

"She played me. I feel like a fool."

"She fooled her twin. She's good. You didn't stand a chance."

"Her twin isn't a homicide detective trained in deception."

"Dad, don't beat yourself up. I think everything has played out the way it was intended. Once I get the photos, let's get together for the next steps. I'll tell you all about my meeting with James and Rob's mom. Okay?"

"Okay."

"Now, don't be a slacker. Finish stacking those chairs."

He laughed. It was good to see him smile again.

Chapter 26

Vicky called a staff meeting to discuss the next steps. Mike picked up breakfast tacos from It's All That and A Cracked Egg. I placed a carafe of coffee on the conference table with a few ceramic cups. Mike walked in, set the taco bag down, and grabbed his bounty hunter coffee mug from the table. It had 'You're Coming with Me' on the top and 'World's Best Bounty Hunter' on the bottom. Vicky reached for her psychic mug with the words 'They're Telling Me' on top and 'Stay in Bed' on the bottom. In the center was a picture of a person in bed with the covers pulled over their head. I handed Rita her remote viewer's mug with an image of a map and a GPS position pin in the map's center.

I filled my World's Greatest PI mug with 'There You Are' on the bottom.

I put salsa and jalapeños on my taco and sat down.

Vicky connected my tablet to the projector's Bluetooth.

"The photos of the jewelry are in the folder called 'Perils R Us.' It's the name of the Insurance carrier."

Vicky clicked on a few of the photos.

"These pieces of jewelry belonged to Mrs. Baxter. They were taken from the safe the night of the murder. I say taken and not stolen because we believe that Maxine took them from the safe to make it look like a robbery." Mike and Rita looked confused.

"Sorry, should've started with I visited the Baxter mansion and saw an imprint of his daughter kill him. You weren't at the session yesterday, but James confirmed it was a life contract between them. He doesn't want to help solve the case, but he won't cause us any trouble. Nick is going to try to run down some photos of Maxine wearing the jewelry after the murder."

"Nick?" Mike asked with a raised eyebrow and a smile.

"I tell you Maxine killed her father and that's your take away? Nick? You know who Nick is. Don't be a third-grader."

"You always called him the Captain. I didn't realize you had shifted to first names." His grin spread even further.

"He's not my boss anymore, and he asked me to call him Nick. Don't read anything into it."

He held up both hands. "Didn't mean to ruffle your feathers."

"You didn't... oh for heaven's sake, stop grinning like that."

He took his hand and swiped it over his face. When his hand lowered, he had a serious look. "This better?"

"You really are a third-grader. Yes, it's better. Anyway, once we get proof of her wearing the jewelry, we'll try for a warrant. My guess is she has them in the house, maybe even the gun."

"Do you have any photos of Maxine's mom?" Mike asked.

"Maxine's mom?" Rita asked.

I knew exactly where he was going with that question. "That's a great idea. If we have photos of both women wearing the same pieces, it'll prove the robbery was faked. There isn't any in the case file, but I'm sure I can pull photos from social sites," I said.

"Can you drop the jewelry photos to my folder?" Rita asked.

"Sure, why?

"I usually remote view by holding objects. I thought I'd try connecting by working with the photos. Maybe I can pick up images of their surroundings."

"That would be awesome. If we could have a location, we could add that to the search warrant."

"I'm not promising anything, but if I get a hit, I'll drop you my drawings."

"I appreciate your trying."

"What do you need from me?" Mike asked.

"Can you trail Maxine? I'm not sure if she is suspicious. I kinda weirded out when I saw her kill James. I may have played it off by saying the wine went to my head, but it's possible she saw right through that. I'd barely finished the glass. I'll drop the address in your work file."

"Sure. No problem. How long should I follow her?"

"Until we get a warrant to search the place."

"Is that everything?" Vicky asked.

"I want to run something totally off-topic by you guys."

"As in not case-related or not related to the jewelry?" Mike asked.

"As in not related to this case or any case, but related to the structure of the agency."

"Go on," Vicky said.

"I'm still in awe of Dad's connection with Mom and Rob's message from his dad. I mean the way Rob broke down, it was like an emotional dam broke from the deepest part of him. Getting permission to walk away from the company with no guilt. It's like a second lease on life for Rob and Sharon. And Dad's letter to mom. What a blessing to be able to get that off his chest. His guilt for not being there for mom after my brother died all gone. I healed, as well. I always thought he abandoned me growing up since he shut me out. Reading his letter, I realized he fought the urge to join them because of me. Had we not set that meeting in motion, I may have never learned that."

"I do feel blessed to have witnessed and held space for all of that to happen," Vicky agreed.

"What if..." I took the time to make eye contact with each one. When I was sure they were fully engaged, I continued. "What if we do that for everyone?"

"What do you mean?" Rita asked.

"If someone wants to connect with a loved one, we make it happen."

"Hello, I've been doing that for years with readings," Vicky said.

"Sure, with readings, but not what we just did with Dad. He actually got to speak to mom in person. Well, as in-person as you can get. Let's stream the souls of anyone that wants closure. Not just victims of murder."

"You're willing to leave your body for strangers? Need I remind you of the fiasco with Sarah? The soul you traded with refused to let you back in. I'm surprised to hear you even contemplate this," Vicky said.

"I know. But. I think it is a great way to give back. To be of service. To balance the horrible things we see people do to each other and bring closure to families. We can let spirits join in on defining moments one last time."

"Join in on defining moments? What are you talking about?" Mike asked.

"This is where it gets crazy," I said.

"Oh, *that's where it gets crazy*, not the part where we fully stream anyone with a message?" Vicky said.

"Yeah, you've got to be careful here. What if someone wants to get something off their chest and the spirit channeled doesn't accept the message or, worse, says something horrible to the person trying to ask for forgiveness. Either way, the spirit could turn on the confessor, or the spirit wanting forgiveness gets slammed down. It could do irreparable damage to the person asking for forgiveness," Rita said.

Mike ran his fingers through his hair. "That's right. I have a friend whose dad was dying. They were estranged for decades because my friend is gay, and his dad could never accept it. On his death bed, he asked my friend to come to see him. My friend thought his dad would apologize and they would resolve things before he died. The opposite happened. His dad asked him to lean in to hear the message. When he did, his dad spat on him and called him a string of horrible names and told him he hated him and was glad his son would be in hell and he would never have to see him again. You can imagine how that destroyed my friend."

"I think his dad will be the one in hell. What an a-hole," Rita said.

"Jeez. I concur with Rita," Vicky said.

"You have to consider the psyche as well. A person has to be strong. It's hard enough to lose a loved one the first time. You are asking them to do it twice. The soul can't stay for any length of time without imprinting to the host. You're going to let someone spend time with a deceased loved one for a what did you call it? A defining moment? Then make them say good-bye all over again? I don't think many people can handle that. You need to make sure that person is stable and knows the good-bye is very much a part of the experience. I think the idea of streaming anyone who wants to share a message is dangerous," Rita said.

"I get it. But that's the thing. Maybe they didn't get to say good-bye. Maybe the death was sudden or the family member couldn't get to them in time before the person died or for some reason chose not to see them before they died and now they are filled with regret," I said.

"My group has been practicing with full streaming for a few years now to help with investigations. It would give the practice an entirely new focus and wouldn't be restricted to crime victims. I can see the joy it would bring amidst all the depravity."

"I wish my mom could have been there for my almost wedding. If she attended via streaming, who knows how my life would have turned out," I said.

"I wish my dad could have walked me down the aisle," Rita added.

"My wife wishes her mom could have visited to help out with the birth of our firstborn. She was convinced she didn't know what she was doing and was going to end up killing our baby," Mike laughed. "Seriously, it would have meant the world to her to have her mom hold our son."

"Then it's settled. This is a good thing. We can call the sub-agency Defining Moments," I said.

"You've got to slow your roll there, sister," Vicky said.

"Slow my what?"

"We need rules. The world's going to see this as the streaming soul's Zombie Apocalypse. We need to limit exposure, and our clients will need to sign a waiver of non-disclosure. We need to make sure both parties are in agreement and both are stable. The only way I can get comfortable around this is to reach out to the clients I have been working with for years. I know which ones would be open to this and have an idea of their stability," Vicky said.

"You pick the people we stream?" Mike said.

"We all pick. I'll reach out to my clients. Those interested can write an essay as to why they should receive a special "streaming" session. I'll gather the papers, and we pick the winner as a team."

"I love it," Rita said.

"This is really going to work. I'm so excited. Thanks, guys. You won't regret it. Vicky, I think we ask for photos of the deceased as well. There are plenty of people on your team I think would be willing to rotate as hosts for their practice. It would be cool to have the host look as close to the deceased as possible to enhance the experience."

"Or make them lose it," Mike said.

"Okay, that will be an interview question. Do you want someone that looks like your loved one," I said.

"I'll get started and gather the essays," Vicky said.

Chapter 27

Paul agreed to help find photos of Maxine and her mom wearing the jewelry. He was excited about another live pilot of his program. He said he would place both a date stamp and the location at the bottom right of each photo. I airdropped shots of the jewelry, a family photo, and an individual photo of Maxine and one of her mom I'd pulled from an old article. He agreed it was a great idea to pull in photos of Maxine's mom wearing the jewelry.

Paul could have arranged for me to pick up the photos but, instead, he invited me to join him and Nick for a few beers. We met at a pub called Legacy. The walls were plastered with photos of local celebrities and news articles of local heroes. They were both laughing when I walked up to the booth. Both had an empty beer bottle in front of them and were working on their second.

Nick jumped up and hugged me. Paul started to stand, but I motioned him to stay seated. He was squeezed into the booth, and I didn't want him to struggle to get out. The table was jabbing him in the stomach. Nick stepped aside from the booth to let me slide in.

"After you," he said.

"You first, I have a tiny bladder. I'll be hitting the lady's room before I finish my beer."

Nick sat down and scooted to make room for me. An open envelope was on the table. It was obvious they had viewed the photos and discussed the case while waiting for me.

I pointed to it. "Looks like you got a head start. You were successful then?"

"Did you have any doubt, Ms. Katie?"

"Not for a second."

I looked through a dozen photos of Maxine and her mom.

"I have a boatload more, but I think these are the best."

I pulled out a report with photos placed above a timeline. "You created a timeline?"

"That I did."

"You're an above-and-beyond kinda guy. Thanks."

"That's how I roll."

"Hum. She didn't start wearing the jewelry until a few years after the murder."

"I bet if you asked your dad when the case went cold, the timing would be the same," he said.

"In Dad's eyes, it was never a cold case. It was always on his mind."

"He may have never given up, but we did pull it from the active list. It was before my time, so I'm not sure when it happened. I'll check tomorrow," Nick said.

"Thanks," I said.

Paul took a swig from his bottle and, before setting it down, said, "Look closely at the photos and the locations. What do you see?"

"I'm not sure about the rest of the photos you have, but she's alone in each of these shots. The photos I found of her on the social sites, she's always dressed to the hilt. In these, her outfits are casual. No business suits, no fancy dresses. Jeans, t-shirts, and shorts. They're low key shots, like she's running errands."

"Right. The one you're holding is from an ATM."

I picked up another. "She's shopping at a grocery store in this one. A three-string pearl necklace is the perfect accessory to jeans and flip flops. The store's security cam? I'm guessing."

"Yep." He pointed to another one on the table. "This one is perfect. One pearl necklace looks like another. Here she's wearing a unique coin necklace." He placed a photo of Maxine's mom wearing the same necklace. A gold coin had an image of a deer standing next to a fawn. He placed two more photos side by side. The necklace they both wore was a large amber stone with a silver wire wrapping around the entire stone.

"This one's the money shot. This amber necklace is a natural stone, with an irregular shape and," he pointed to the top corner, "it has a plant inclusion. We can have an expert testify to the pattern in both photos. If she tries to say she replicated her mom's jewelry, there would be no way she could find a matching stone."

"Look at you, Mr. Gemologist," I said.

"I can't take credit. I showed it to an expert. He's working on an appraisal for you."

"Thanks."

"You're welcome. You'll be getting a bill," he said.

"That's fine. I appreciate your jumping on it."

"What else do you see?"

I stared at the photos.

"Look at the date stamp."

I spread them out. "The most recent one is a few weeks before I started calling her. She stopped when she found out the case was active again!"

"I have hundreds of photos, just like this. She was careful not to wear the jewelry around anyone and stopped when she thought she might be watched."

Nick added, "It's an ego trip. She got away with murder and wearing the jewelry as a reminder of her victory."

"I think it's deeper."

They looked at me.

"It makes her feel close to her mom. It's not about her ego. I bet when she is wearing clothes that do not reveal her neckline, she's wearing them under her clothes."

Nick pointed to my cross necklace. "I take it, that's your mom's?"

"I put my hand around it. "It is."

I looked at Paul. "It's what gave me the idea to have you search your database."

He held up the photo with the amber necklace. "It was genius-level thinking, whatever the trigger."

"That's my Katie," Nick said.

"Your Katie?" I asked.

He blushed. "You know what I mean."

Paul looked pleased with our exchange. It made me wonder if he was playing match-maker when he invited me for drinks.

Chapter 28

Rob and Sharon invited me to dinner. I rang the doorbell and held up a bottle of Merlot in front of the security camera.

Sharon opened the door and hugged me. "You didn't have to do that."

"But I did. Mom taught me never to show up empty-handed."

Rob walked up, and I handed him the bottle. "Thank your mom for me."

"I certainly will."

"Come in. Dinner will be ready in a few."

I followed Sharon to the living room. Rob veered off to the kitchen.

I sat down on a loveseat. "Beautiful home."

"Thanks. It's small compared to Maxine's place, but we wouldn't trade our love nest for anything."

Rob returned, holding three empty wine glasses in one hand, and the open bottle in the other. He set the glasses on the coffee table, poured a small amount, swirled it, and offered it to me.

I wasn't a fine wine drinker but decided to go through the motions. I laughed, taking it and repeated the swirl, breathed in the wine, took a sip, and let it roll across my tongue. I handed it back. "Fill 'er up. It's not worthy of Maxine's wine cellar but has a smooth taste. I hope you guys will like it."

Rob put a few ounces in each glass. He handed Sharon hers, returned mine, and took a sip from his. "It's perfect. Thanks."

Sharon tried hers and set the glass down. "It's delicious. It'll go well with the roast. Speaking of which, I'd better check on it." The kitchen was open to the living room and had a bar stool countertop dividing the two rooms. I walked behind her, sat on a barstool while watching her open the stove to check the temperature. Rob sat down next to me.

"It's ready. Rob, grab the platter."

He jumped up, grabbed a large ceramic dish from an antique hutch, and placed it on the counter. Sharon lifted the roast using a pair of forks and lowered it on the platter.

"It smells amazing," I said.

"I hope it tastes amazing," she said.

Rob picked up the dish. "Shall we?"

"Let's." I followed him to the dining area.

We were halfway through the meal when Rob brought up the case.

"On the phone, you said you had a break."

We were having such a pleasant, relaxing evening, I'd almost forgotten about the reason for the visit.

"Rob, Sharon, I..." My hands went clammy. A cold sweat formed on my brow. My mouth was so dry my tongue felt like beef jerky.

"Are you okay? You just went pale. Is it the red wine again?" he asked.

I swallowed hard. "No, I should have given more detail on the phone. I don't know how to say this."

Rob sat back in his chair. Sharon stood next to him, placing her hand on his shoulder.

"What is it?" she asked.

I locked my eyes on Rob's. "Are you familiar with life contracts?"

Sharon nodded. "It's an agreement we make before we're born to share a life with the same people across lifetimes."

Rob added, "We take turns being family members, even sexes, to see things from each other's perceptive."

"Right, and we agree to events or behaviors based on our past actions," I said.

"Karma," Sharon said.

"Karma," Rob echoed.

"Maxine and your dad had an agreement in this lifetime. An agreement your dad understands and feels he deserved."

"What are you saying?"

"I'm sorry to have to say this, but Maxine is responsible for your dad's death. Unfortunately, she won't remember it was because of a contractual agreement with your dad. Our memories of any agreements erase the moment we are born. Only our inner-selves, our soul, remembers."

"Is that what Dad told you?"

"He confirmed it and, at first, he didn't want us to arrest her. But now both your mom and dad understand and agree the arrest must happen. The murder and accountability are what Maxine's soul agreed to on a spiritual level before she was born and would want the arrest to happen if she remembered."

Rob looked up at Sharon. "I was afraid of this."

Sharon nodded and squeezed his shoulder.

"What do you mean?" I asked.

"After we left Maxine's, you asked if it could have been Dad I heard in the background. I dismissed it but kept having dreams about my call with Maxine. I assumed the virtual home assistant was offline and that's why Maxine couldn't get the volume lowered on the TV. I woke up with a start after one of the dreams, realizing if the assistant was offline, the TV would have been off line as well. It was connected to the assistant, that is how the channels were streamed."

"When did you realize this?" I asked.

"A few nights ago. I pushed the thought down. Tried to think of other reasons why the TV would be working without the VR. I tried to remember the sounds to see if I could filter in Dad's voice. I just can't be sure."

"Why didn't you tell me?" I asked.

"I don't want to believe it. If I told you, you would have run with it and arrested her."

"Rob..." I was about to respond when Sharon interjected.

"Why didn't you tell us James confirmed Maxine killed him after the session?" she asked, frowning in my direction.

"I wanted to test out a theory first."

"What theory?"

"We uncovered photos of Maxine wearing your mom's jewelry."

"She used to wear Mom's jewelry all the time. It's no big deal," Rob said.

"The photos we found were taken after your dad died, after the robbery."

Rob put his head in his hands. "My sister did this so I would inherit the money; it's what Maxine was implying on the phone that night. My dream was real. Dad was in the background. He was alive. I could've stopped it."

"You couldn't have. Maxine did this. Because on some level, her subconscious recalled the agreement. She may have thought it would benefit you, but that's not why it happened. All of you agreed to this before you were born. Your mom, you, Maxine, and your dad. Don't blame yourself."

He looked up and placed his hands on the table. "What happens now?"

"We're going to show the judge the photos and see if we can get a warrant. We hoped to expedite the search by having Rita remote view the jewelry. Unfortunately, she couldn't get a read from the photos. The only thing that came through was that the jewelry was in darkness. The viewing was incomplete because she was working from a photo instead of an object. It wasn't possible to zoom out to see the surroundings. They must be in a box or buried."

"It's a book," Rob said.

"What's a book?"

"The jewelry isn't buried in a box. I bet it's in a carved-out book we used to hide our weed from Dad. The book is *Touching the Cosmos*. It's still on the bookcase. I saw it when we were at the house. I almost made a joke but thought Maxine would be upset if you knew she smoked weed."

"Rob, thank you. I won't include that in the warrant. I don't want Maxine to know you helped. You need to be there for her. She's not going to understand going to prison is part of the bigger picture. It's for her spiritual growth, and serving time will erase the karmic debt between your dad and Maxine. Your next rotation as a family is going to be an amazing beautiful life for you all."

"I hope you're right that what's about to happen is going to change the trajectory of our lives." Rob's shoulders hunched. "Can you ask for leniency?"

"I can't explain it's because of a contractual agreement."

Rob brushed tears from his eyes.

"I'll get with the team. I promise we'll come up with something."

Chapter 29

I was emotionally and physically spent. I fed Cooper, tossed him the ball a few times, and was ready to call it a night. I grabbed my tablet and climbed into bed. One quick email to the team with a summary of the evening, and I'd be off to dreamland. My commitment to Rob to develop something to plead leniency for Maxine felt like a weighted blanket.

Would leniency lessen the spiritual growth she signed up for in this lifetime? I thought of God's grace and the Lord's Prayer. "Forgive us our trespasses as we forgive those who trespass against us." Then my thoughts shifted to "turn the other cheek." Could we return a harmful act with a kind one and absolve this? Is an eye for an eye necessary? James forgave Maxine. Was it possible to consider the karmic chain broken and leave the case unsolved? No. That would leave Sabrina in jail for a crime she didn't commit. We had to see this through.

I put the tablet on the nightstand and rested my head on the pillow. Within seconds, I had a strange sensation of falling into the bed. I was whisked into a deep sleep and slammed into a lucid dream. I was aware of the scene unfolding in my mind and, thanks to Cooper's weight against my leg, aware I was asleep. I tried to shake off the uneasy feeling of how quickly I had fallen asleep and focused on the dream.

I was in a baseball game and up at-bat. *I don't watch baseball. Why am I dreaming about baseball? This has to be a sign! Remember this dream when you wake up. Remember this dream when you wake up.* I repeated the phrase a few times. Vicky taught me this when I first started having lucid dreams.

I raised the bat and looked at the pitcher. My heart skipped a beat when I recognized Nick on the pitcher's mound. I tightened my grip on the bat and looked behind me. Vicky was the catcher and Paul was the home-plate umpire. My eyes scanned the field. Maxine was on first base and Rob was on second. I raised my hand to block out the sun and looked toward the stands. A few people were watching the game. Dad was high in the bleachers, waving. I waved back before realizing he was waving at the hot dog vendor with a metal hot dog box. "Get your hot dogs! Cold drinks, hot peanuts! Get your hot dogs!"

"Play Ball" boomed from the loudspeakers. My head snapped towards Nick to make sure there wasn't a fastball flying at me. Our eyes connected. He looked right and left, raised his leg, and threw the ball. My breath caught in my chest. I swung and made contact, threw the bat, and ran full speed, as did Rob and Maxine. The ball rolled a few feet past second. The second baseman grabbed the ball and missed tagging Maxine, sliding into second. I was safe on first, and Rob stretched out with a hand on third. Paul pointed to Maxine, shouted "Safe," and with his hands motioned safe. He did this several times. I wondered why he made the call more than once. No one seemed to question it. I woke up as quickly as I had fallen asleep.

I sat up, threw the covers off, grabbed my tablet, opened the messaging app. *Paul, Vicky, Rick, please meet me for breakfast at 'It's All That and A Cracked Egg' around 7:30. Agenda: Help to interpret the weirdest dream ever. You were all in it. Before breakfast, please noodle on your role in the dream. I laid out the dream's details. For obvious reasons, I'm leaving Max and Rob off of the invite. Please think of Dad's role in the stands. I'm weighing inviting him. If he shows up, you'll know which way I leaned.*

Chapter 30

I was the first one to arrive and requested a table for four. I didn't invite Dad. That he was in the stands made me decide he should remain on the periphery until we ironed out the meaning. There were several open tables. I pointed to a back corner as the hostess grabbed the menus.

"Can you tuck us back there?"

"No problem." She marked an x over her electronic seating chart. "Follow me."

I sat with my back to the wall so I could wave when everyone walked in.

She handed me my menu and laid out the remaining. "Your server is George. He'll be over in a moment to get your coffee going."

"Did my dark circles give away the long night I had?"

"You look great, sugar. Tired is all."

"I'm more than a bit tired. George may need to leave the pot."

She smiled. "I'll give him a heads-up."

Nick was the first to arrive. He honed in on me. Vicky was right behind him. They both moved through the tables like they were racing.

"Morning, guys. Take a seat. I really appreciate you meeting me before work."

"Morning." Vicky plopped down. "I'd never turn down an opportunity for a breakfast taco. Glad you had that wacky dream."

"Morning." Nick sat across from me. "Paul sent me a text. He's stuck at the light one street up. He said to order him the sunrise platter."

I nodded, not the least bit surprised Paul would have a hefty appetite. The special was enough to feed all of us.

George walked over, holding a carafe, and poured three cups. I pointed to Paul's setting. "Fill that one as well. He's stuck at the light around the corner. We've got his order if you're ready to take it."

"Fire away."

We each placed our orders. He didn't document the requests. "Shouldn't take long." He set the carafe on the table. Wave if you need more. I heard you had a long night." He winked like I had stayed up all night partying.

Nick grinned. "Tie one on at Rob and Sharon's last night?"

"No. Dinner ended early after I dropped the bomb that Maxine killed Rob's dad. The dark circles are from tossing and turning all night after the dream."

"Did Rob freak out?" Vick asked.

"No. Just the opposite. He had already figured it out. He kept thinking about my hint she was involved and realized it was James in the background, not the TV."

"Great. We can use that in the warrant," Nick said.

"We can't. I'm going to leave him out for now. He's not 100% confident. He recalled Maxine kept telling the virtual assistant to turn down the TV, which didn't work. He figured the virtual assistant was offline. He realized if the assistant were out of commission, the TV would have been as well. He's pretty broken up. He told me the jewelry might be in a book they had hollowed-out to hide weed. Can you get a warrant from Paul's timeline of Maxine wearing the jewelry? Just put the den in the warrant. I don't want Maxine to know Rob is helping. Tell the team to search for the book 'Touching the Cosmos.'"

"It shouldn't be a problem. I'll get something worked up today and tell the team about the book."

"Thanks."

Paul weaved to our table. He had to stand sideways between the tables to get through. A few customers had to scoot their chairs in to let him through. Let's just say he wouldn't have won the race Nick and Vicky ran. He pulled back the empty chair and sat down. "Sorry I'm late. What did I miss?"

Nick brought him up to speed.

"Thanks for coming, Paul. You were the umpire in the dream and very adamant in calling Maxine safe. I mimicked the call sign for safe. In fact, you repeated the call several times. Am I correct there is no need to repeat the call?"

"You're correct," Nick said.

"I was thinking before bed we should drop the case. James has forgiven Maxine, and Rob understands why it happened. It seemed like a good idea until I remembered Sabrina. It's not right to let her take the blame. I'm not sure Sabrina would win in court. The evidence is stacked against her."

"So, how is Maxine safe if we have to arrest her?" Vicky asked.

"If they drop the case?" I said hopefully.

"You mean, Your Honor, we respectfully ask you to drop the case. It was a life contract, after all? I get life contracts, but I don't see that happening," Vicky said.

"There's no way that's happening," Nick agreed.

"Looks like we're two for two," Paul said.

"Two for two?" I asked.

"Two metaphysical peeps on the team and two analytical," he said.

"I resent that. Let's say two and one-half analytical. I still have detective blood running through my veins," I said.

"Okay, I resent that. There's nothing wrong with being metaphysical," Vicky pouted.

"You're right. There's nothing wrong with being on the woo-woo side. But let me take a stab at it from the analytical side," Paul said.

"Go ahead. What does safe mean to you?" I asked.

"I'm literal. A safe means just that. A safe to lock away valuables."

"Let's break down everything we know about the safe," Nick said.

"It's biometric and opened by fingerprint. Only Maxine and James had profiles that opened the safe. The killer cut James' finger off to open the safe, but that doesn't mean

Maxine didn't cut it off to make it appear like a robbery," I said.

"I'll tell you what I know about biometric safes. For security reasons, fingerprints aren't stored on the network. They're stored in a separate unit in the safe. What's stored on the network is entry and activity logs," Paul said.

"Do you know if your dad accessed the logs?" Nick asked.

"It wasn't in the file. I don't think so. Dad's not geared toward technology. When he saw the cut finger, there was no doubt how the safe was opened. I'm not sure I would've questioned it either," I said.

"Wait," Vicky said.

We all looked at her. She squirmed in her chair, excited.

"Using my analytical side," she paused.

"I meant nothing bad by that," Paul apologized.

"It's okay. I'm giving you a hard time. Katie, do you remember when you told me the killer cut the finger off to open the safe, and I said, ouch?"

"Yes."

"Do you remember what you said?"

"Don't worry, the murderer cut it off after he was dead."

"Close enough," Vicky said, pausing for what seemed dramatic affect.

"Holy crap," I responded.

Both Paul and Nick asked, "What?"

"According to the autopsy, James was already dead when his finger was amputated. It wasn't used to break into the safe. It was used to cover up the fact that Maxine had opened the safe," I said.

"I'm not following," Paul said.

"Maxine used her finger to open the safe to get the gun out. She killed him, then cut off his finger to throw off the fact that she opened the safe. She must have realized the program would log her fingerprint, so she cut his finger off to cover up the fact that she opened the safe," I said.

Vicky nodded. "Yep, that's where I was going."

"Paul, can you hack the system and confirm the entry log?" I asked.

"With my eyes closed, but you don't want me to do that."

"I don't?"

"This is the nail on the coffin. The proverbial smoking gun. You need to do this right. You want the forensics team to find this. There are two separate logs. You have entry logs and diagnostic logs. The diagnostic runs every 24 hours and records up to 1,000 entries. If James scheduled a backup, it would generate a new file once it logs a thousand diagnostics. This is true for the entry log. Most people only access their safe every few years. It isn't something you go in and out of. I'm guessing the initial profile hasn't hit a thousand entries, even after 20 years. If it has, you'd better cross your fingers a backup schedule was set up. I can walk the forensic IT guys through it if they need help."

"They should be able to handle it. I'll give them your number as back up," Nick said.

"Nick, can you add the safe and the network to the warrant?" I asked.

"Like you need to ask?" he said.

"Sorry, I know you're on top of it. Thanks."

George brought our plates on one giant tray and laid each one in front without asking who ordered what. His memory was impressive.

"It smells delicious. Thanks, George," I said.

He picked up the carafe. "I'll come back with a fresh one."

"Thanks, man," Nick said.

I picked up my fork to dig in. Nick stared at his plate.

"Isn't that what you ordered?" I asked.

"Your dad won't take this well. It's a big miss. He would've solved this case immediately if he weren't so scared of technology."

I put down my fork. "We're going to have to play up that all of us might've made the same assumption. You've got a severed finger and an open safe. Why would you question how it was opened? Honestly, like I said earlier, I'm not sure I would've dug deeper."

Chapter 31

Nick was successful in obtaining a warrant to include the diagnostic records for the safe. As Paul predicted, there were less than 1,000 log entries for the access records. We didn't bother with the diagnostics. The team made a deliberate mess of opening every book on the bookshelf and dropping them as to avoid the appearance of having prior knowledge of the hollowed-out book.

Just as Rob described, *Touching the Cosmos* contained the stolen jewelry in the carved-out center. As instructed, Mike, the bounty hunter, had been following Maxine and was on standby to advise of her location for the arrest.

Dad, not yet retired, was still the detective assigned to the case. I was only assisting in an unofficial capacity as a private investigator. Dad would have the honor of obtaining the arrest warrant, serving it, and bringing Maxine into custody. I say honor but wasn't sure he'd feel the same. Maxine and Dad had gotten close, and Dad was still struggling to see Sabrina as falsely accused.

I decided this was a job for a hot burger and chocolate shake. I gave Dad a heads-up I was stopping by with lunch and had new details to update. I was armed with his favorite meal, photos of the jewelry, and the log from the safe showing Maxine's fingerprint had opened it ten minutes before James' fingerprint. Maxine and James had the only two profiles that could open it.

With the log entry, it was clear that the safe was opened before James' death with Maxine's print. The safe was later closed and, within seconds of closing, reopened with James' fingerprint. Dad couldn't deny Maxine had murdered her father. As was the usual pattern for get-togethers at the house, Dad had the front door slightly cracked for my arrival. I knew it was a signal to walk right in, but I still rapped my knuckles against the frame.

"Dad? I'm here." I walked in closing the door behind me.

"In the kitchen!"

He was setting two plates on the table and pointed to the takeout bag. "Bring that puppy over here. My mouth has been watering since the moment you called."

"For the burger or shake?"

"Both!"

I placed the two shakes on the table and loaded a burger and fries on each plate. I dumped the ketchup packets on the center of the table. Dad was already sitting and peeling the wrapper from his burger.

"Hungry?"

"Starving. My appetite goes through the roof when I'm about to get hit with heavy news."

"What do you mean? I... I only mentioned that I needed to bring you up to speed on the case. I didn't share any of the details."

"Burger and chocolate shake with the update? It's your tell. Don't ever play poker."

"Ah. I didn't think I was that obvious."

"Hit me. I'm sitting and enjoying my favorite meal. What do ya got for me?"

I pulled my tablet from my purse, showed him the jewelry photos, and opened an image of the safe's log showing the page from the date of death. Both Maxine's and James's entries were highlighted. I said nothing as he stared at the log.

He furrowed his brow as he read. The edge of his ears turned red. He cleared his throat. "How was this obtained? Did you do it right? Can we use this?"

"We did it by the book. Everything is from a legal search warrant. We've got her, Dad."

He pushed his plate away.

"Dad, hear me out. This is good news. Nick's leaving the arrest warrant to you. Mike's tailing Maxine and can give us her location so you can make the arrest and bring her in."

He shoved the tablet across the table. "Give it to a cop. I didn't solve this case. I kept it from being solved. I believed her. I didn't even know a safe could log activity. Worse, I arrested the wrong person. I never listened to you. I didn't trust your instincts. Don't make a mockery of me with this charade like I solved this case. I'll be a laughing stock at the department. It's all I'll be remembered for after I retire."

"No." I pushed the tablet back to his side of the table. "Nick, Paul, and I talked about it. We would've handled the case the same. Why would anyone assume the safe was opened any other way? The finger was cut off and the safe was open. No reason to think otherwise."

"So, you all sat around and had a good laugh about how to placate the old dinosaur?"

"That's not how it happened. None of us would have gone there if it hadn't been for my dream."

He raised an eyebrow. "Dream?"

I laid out the entire dream to include his part in the stand.

"See, I'm in the stands, not part of the game, not part of the case, and not part of the arrest."

"I don't think that is why you were in the stands, Dad."

"Enlighten me."

I still hadn't figured it out but needed to come up with something. I closed my eyes and looked up, hoping to activate the frontal lobe, the thinking part of my brain. It was a meditation technique Vicky taught me to problem solve. I saw a smoky purple haze which relaxed me. I opened my eyes.

"You were in the stands because you're about to retire. You asked me to help solve the case, remember? That was your choice. Baseball is about catching and throwing. You had the ball and threw it to me. You trusted me to be on your team. Being in the stands versus on the field means you're satisfied. You're trusting the flow of the investigation."

"And the hot dog guy? I'm just sitting back stuffing my face, enjoying the show?"

That one was harder. "Uh, think of the hot dog as representing a real dog, like Cooper. Dogs are loyal and protective by nature. This particular hot dog represents your loyalty to the case, your protection of James, and bringing his killer to justice."

"You really think so?"

"I do. This is *your* case. See it through. Let's get the warrant going and bring her in. Get her to tell you why she did it. Maybe on some level she can give us something we can use to lighten her sentence."

"She's a killer. I feel bad she lost her mom at a young age, but she's still a killer. You lost your mom and didn't kill anyone. Why do you want her sentence reduced?"

"I promised Rob I would think of something. He feels guilty that she may have killed James to keep him from cutting Rob out of the will. He feels responsible. James was alive in the background when Maxine called. He could hear him but thought it was the TV. If he had paid closer attention to the sound, he thinks he could've talked Maxine out of it. I also know the murder is because of an agreement she made with James before being born."

"That's not extenuating circumstances that would weigh in her favor. '"Your Honor, my client killed her father but only out of love for her brother and the desire he maintains the lifestyle in which he had grown accustomed. Plus, your Honor, her dad wanted to be murdered.'"

"Speaking from experience, twins share a protective bond. Maybe we can get an expert witness to attest that such a bond can cause irrational behavior if a twin is threatened or is perceived to be threatened."

"I don't know what else we can use," he said.

"Just be the good guy when you arrest her. Get her to talk freely. Something will come up from her subconscious, her inner soul. If you ask direct questions, her soul will shut down. Let it happen organically by telling her how sorry you are that she lost her mom at such a young age. Let her know you understand her need to protect her brother."

"You're really in to this soul and contract stuff, aren't you?"

"I am. I learned so much when I crossed over. It's bleeding into how I see our lives unfolding, why we're here, why we do the things we do. At least I'm dipping my toe in the water. There's so much to learn."

"I'm sorry I reacted like I didn't appreciate your solving this case. I wanted it solved before I retired and wanted you to be the one to solve it. On some level, I thought if you used the psychic stuff, I wouldn't look bad for not solving it. Instead, you used technology to prove she was still wearing her mom's jewelry and technology to link her to the safe."

"Need I remind you the link to the safe was generated from a dream? That's psychic stuff. My vision at the mansion of Maxine killing James couldn't be more psychic. The technology I used to find the photos of Maxine wearing the jewelry wasn't around when you were investigating. P-Kate's clues..." I stuttered. *Dad didn't know about P-Kate.*

"P-Kate's clues?"

"Uh, that's what I call clues from my dreams. I call my inner soul, P-Kate. Our soul has full memory of our agreements, our mission in this lifetime, and a memory of all lifetimes. With meditation, I've learned to listen to guidance from P-Kate." That was all true. My inner soul was connected and aligned to all parallel fragments of me; receiving clues via dreams was part of that connection.

"What's the P stand for?"

I can't say, parallel-world Kate. "Uh, P stands for.... for, uh... personification Kate."

"Sounds heavy."

"She personifies my soul, my higher-self. She's an embodiment of my inner knowing." *Wow, that was fast. I like it. It works.*

"Can't deny you're tapped into something. You should have stayed a homicide detective. You'd have one heck of a closing ratio."

"I'm right where I need to be. I'll still be helping and closing cases. Don't you worry about that. So, you'll request the warrant and make the arrest?"

"Yes."

"Before you do that, can you ask the DA to drop the charges against Sabrina? I'd like to have her released as soon as possible and back with her family."

"Of course, I'm so sorry I didn't listen to you."

"I'm not the one you owe the apology."

"I owe it to both of you."

"Apology accepted from me. Call the DA now, and that will be a step in the right direction for Sabrina."

"Can I finish my burger?"

"Of course. I hope it's not too cold."

I've never seen anyone chew so slowly. It was one of his favorite burgers. Even if it was cold, he was savoring every bite. He finally finished and took a few slow sips from his shake. He seemed to enjoy my agony. It seemed like an eternity before he took out his phone, put it on speaker, and hit speed dial.

Chapter 32

Vicky and Rita were waiting in the conference room for an early celebration. I wanted to personally congratulate them on closing the case. I didn't think celebrating was premature, even though we still had to get Sabrina released and Maxine arrested. They both stood and clapped when I walked in. I took a bow.

"Now pat yourselves on the back. We solved our first case together." Rita and Vicky laughed and patted each other on the back.

"Where's Mike?" Rita asked.

"He's keeping an eye on Maxine and is fully briefed. Dad's prepping an arrest warrant based on the stolen jewelry and the safe's log. The charge is murder. He won't have any trouble getting it. I imagine she will be arrested tonight or first thing in the morning."

"Does Rob know?" Rita asked

"I called him after I listened in on Dad's conversation with the DA."

"Sounds like it went well if we are high-fiving," Vicky said.

"It did. The DA agreed the evidence exonerates Sabrina, and he's working on her release. Dad's filling out the affidavit for the arrest warrant. Technically, we could arrest Maxine and then have the judge determine probable cause soon after the arrest, but with Mike hawk-eying her, she's not a flight risk. We want to take the time to seal the deal upfront. Speaking of Mike, let me put him on speaker."

I raised my phone, activating the virtual assistant. "Call Mike."

"Hello?" Mike answered on the first ring.

"This a good time? Are you near Maxine?"

"Yeah, I'm in my car watching her office window. She's been on calls all day. What's up?"

"Filling in the team on the next steps and wanted you on the line."

"Appreciate it."

"Katie, are you going to be there when she's arrested?" Vicky asked.

"I hope so. Technically, I'm not part of the department. We're hoping she won't put up a fight. Maybe Dad can get her to confess so it won't be a long, drawn-out trial and, hopefully, if she confesses, her sentence will be reduced."

"I'm still wrapping my head around wanting to help her but, if that's the case, you might want to rethink that strategy," Mike said.

"Trying to get her to confess?"

"Yeah, it might not lead to anything. A confession is a slam-dunk for the DA. What's the incentive to bargain if he has a confession?"

"It's harder to get a murder conviction. There's no way to prove the gun from the safe was used to kill him. Her having the jewelry could be nothing more than insurance fraud. Her attorney could argue Sabrina shot James with the gun she had in her purse. He could say Maxine freaked out when she came home and saw her dad dead. She opened the safe to get the gun because the murderer might still be in the house. Realizing opening the safe tied her to the gun, she panicked and closed it. To cover, she cut off his finger and opened the safe again so she wouldn't look guilty. She kept the jewelry to add credibility she didn't shoot her dad."

"You think Sabrina is still a suspect?" Mike asked.

"Of course not. I saw Maxine's imprint shoot James. She has the money to hire the best attorney. We don't want Sabrina pulled back in. If we hear what happened that night, why she did it, there's still an opportunity to reduce the sentence with no risk to Sabrina."

"Good point. Was she under an extreme emotional disturbance?" he asked.

"She was emotional about James cutting Rob out of the will," I said.

"Hum. They could ask for a psychological report, but that feels weak. Maybe her attorney could hire a mitigation specialist? Was she acting under compulsion or duress? Diminished capacity? Unusual circumstances? An unexpected jolt of anger or rage? Addiction?" he asked.

"I'm not sure. We're going to need to get her side of it," I said.

"First offense, I'm assuming."

"Yes."

"It's your dad's call but, if it were me, I'd make a soft approach. I'd get the arrest warrant but not go to her for the arrest," Mike said.

"Why?" Rita asked.

"I think she will be less likely to clam up if Katie's dad uses his relationship with her to get her to talk. Instead of making a dramatic arrest at her house or office, he brings her in for questioning about the jewelry and the log. He'd let her know the new evidence doesn't look good for her; he's only trying to help clear things up. Your dad would make her feel like he only wants her to explain it. Of course, he would be upfront that she has the right to have an attorney present because anything she shares can be used against her," Mike said.

"I told Dad to use his relationship with her. It makes sense to have her come in. I think Dad will agree."

"What about Sabrina? When will she be released?" Rita asked.

"Today. There's no reason to hold her once the charges are dropped. I've asked to be notified. I want to be there when she is released."

"Is that a good idea? Doesn't she blame you?" Vicky asked.

"You're right. Those were Sabrina's last words to me. I tried to explain about Dad, but she told me I was responsible and asked to be taken back to her cell."

"You haven't visited since?" Vicky asked.

"No. What else could I say? I was responsible. I had her come in to give her statement."

"She can't blame you. All the evidence pointed directly to her. Plus, she confessed to tying James up," Mike said.

"Tying him up, not killing him," I reminded.

"I think you'd better wait to let her life settle before reaching out again. I get that you want to apologize, but give her some space, some time," Rita said.

"You're right. I'm sure her entire family will be there to pick her up. I don't need to distract from that. The good news is that the story never hit the news. She was lucky she was arrested so close to the presidential election. The only thing that has been on the news for months is the poll stats and who slung mud at who. Thanks to no media coverage, she's still safe from her abusive ex."

"Thank heavens for that," Vicky said.

"Isn't she still married to him? Isn't that illegal?" Mike asked.

"Yes and yes. The DA said to avoid any wrongful arrest lawsuit, no bigamy charges will be brought. Plus, he understood she did it because her life was in danger. He wasn't going to drag her back into the public eye," I said.

"It wasn't a wrongful arrest. There was plenty of evidence for probable cause," Mike said.

"I agree, but that doesn't stop people from suing. I'm glad she works for a law firm. It'll add weight to the decision to let the bigamy go," I said.

Vicky walked over to the conference room credenza and opened the center cabinet. "I've got something we can do while we wait for Maxine's interrogation." She held up a stack of papers.

"What's that?" I asked.

"I can't see. What's what? What's going on?" Mike asked.

"Vicky's holding up a stack of paperwork," Rita shared.

"Not paperwork, essays. Remember, I was tasked with polling my clients to pick a few that might be interested in

Katie's Defining Moments project. I narrowed it down to the top three I'm most confident can handle streaming a loved one who has passed."

She took a few papers from the top and set the stack down. "These three clients are stable, and I connected with each of the spirits invited to a defining moment and am certain they'll honor the terms. They're aware that only one will be selected this first go-round and are on board."

I held my hand out for the essays and did a quick glance. I handed one back to Vicky, gave one to Rita, and kept one for myself. "Let's read each one out loud for Mike and vote. Who wants to start?"

Rita jumped in. "This one's interesting."

Chapter 33

I met Dad at the station. The DA reviewed the arrest warrant and the judge signed it. Maxine agreed to come in to answer a few questions. I wouldn't be allowed to be in the interrogation room, but Nick decided I could watch the interview from the closed-circuit monitor. It was against protocol to let a private investigator watch but, since I assisted with the case and, until recently, I'd been a part of the department, he agreed.

Dad waited with me in the circuit room.

"She should be here any minute," Dad said, looking at his watch. He took out his cell phone and checked to make sure it wasn't on silent.

Movement on the monitor caught my eye. "I know you have to have someone else in the room with you because Maxine is female, but Susan's sitting in with you? I thought you hated her."

"Hate is too strong. She leans very hard on my nerves, but she takes great notes and adds good questions if I get too focused on one topic."

As if on cue, Susan placed her tablet down and took a small water bottle from her pocket. She took a box of tissue from the credenza and placed it on the round table. No other furniture or pictures were in the room to cause a distraction. Four chairs surrounded the round table. Dad's phone rang.

"On my way." He put the phone in his pocket.

"That was the front desk. She's here. I'll go and get her," he said.

"Good luck, Dad."

He didn't say anything but patted my shoulder on the way out. I looked at the monitor. Susan was talking on her cell phone. She hung up and stood next to one of the chairs. She must have received the same call that Maxine was on site. Dad walked in with Maxine. I turned up the volume.

"Have a seat, Maxine. Please have some water if you like," Susan said.

Dad cleared his throat. "Recording on." A red light blinked from the base of the camera hanging from the ceiling. Dad looked straight at the camera and stated the date, time, location, his name, Maxine's name, and Susan's full name.

Maxine didn't appear phased that she was being recorded. She looked at Dad. "You said you had another break in the case? Did Sabrina confess?"

"No. She didn't. We've received some information that is taking the case in a different direction. We wanted you to walk us through the night of the murder."

"Again! What for? I can't relive that night. Please don't make me."

Dad ignored her plea. "We know your fingerprint opened the safe that night. We recovered the jewelry while searching your home. You loved your dad more than anything. If you did this, you had to have a reason. I want to help you but, to do that, I've got to understand what happened."

Maxine cried but made no effort to wipe away the tears.

Dad took a seat and leaned in. "Maxine, before saying anything, I need you to know you can refuse to answer questions and don't have to share information."

Maxine jolted upright and looked over her right shoulder and then her left. She put her hand on her right shoulder as if holding something in place. Her eyes grew wide as she turned her gaze to Dad. "Can you smell that?"

Dad looked startled. "I don't smell anything."

She turned her head slowly toward Susan. "What's the shampoo you use?"

Susan didn't answer.

Maxine slammed her hand on the table. "I need to know. What brand of shampoo do you use?"

Susan looked at Dad. He nodded for her to respond.

"Whatever is on sale. Coconut something this time. Why?"

"Not lavender? Are you sure it wasn't a bottle with lavender? What about the conditioner? Was it lavender?"

"Both were coconut."

Maxine leaned in and sniffed Dad's shirt. "Did you smoke a cigar today?"

He scooted his chair back. "Maxine, no, I didn't. What on earth?"

I grabbed the remote and zoomed in on Maxine. I couldn't see James or his wife, but I knew they were both in the room from her reaction. I didn't have my tablet to warn Dad.

Irritated, Susan put her hand up. "Stop," she said, staring at Dad.

She turned toward Maxine. "Maxine Baker, you have the right to remain silent. Anything you say can be used against you in court. You have the right to an attorney for advice before you answer any questions, and to have your attorney present during questioning. If you can't afford an attorney, one will be appointed for you before any questioning if you wish. If you decide to answer questions without a lawyer present, you have the right to stop at any time."

Blood drained from Maxine's face before Susan had finished the Miranda.

"Do you want to call your lawyer?" Dad asked.

She put her cheek against her shoulder. Did she feel her mom next to her? Was her mom's hand on her shoulder? It was the only explanation.

Maxine sat up straight and cleared her throat. "No."

Dad pointed to the camera. "Remember, you're on record and you're being recorded now. Maxine, are you sure you don't want to talk to your attorney?" Dad asked.

"I'm sure."

"All right, walk us through the evening."

"I was partying with a few of my girlfriends. We mixed ecstasy with way too much alcohol. Laura, one of my friends, started getting paranoid and freaking out about being in public. She kept saying everyone was watching her. I told Julie to take her home. After they left, I danced for a few songs, got bored, and went home."

She stopped talking and stared at the wall. Her eyes widened as if watching something play out in front of her. Dad didn't interfere. Susan wasn't as patient.

"What happened when you got home?" Susan asked.

Maxine looked up at Susan and then over to Dad. "I loved Dad, just like you said."

"I know. What did you come home to?" Dad asked.

"Dad was wiggling on the floor, crying out. I was frozen. I stared at him, trying to figure out who tied him up. I thought I heard something in the hall. I panicked and grabbed the gun from the safe. I looked out in the hall, but no one was there. The gun felt so heavy in my hands. It's like it became a part of my hand. I was high and can't explain it, but I felt one with the gun. Like it was a part of me, it was natural to hold it. I swear I felt my mom touch my shoulder." She put her hand on her shoulder again and looked up. "Like right now. I feel a hand on my shoulder right now!"

"I smelled her lavender shampoo. Just like right now." She looked at Dad and Susan. "You smell it too, right? Lavender and cigars?" Her eyes pleaded with them to say 'Yes.' They shook their heads and instinctively looked around the room.

"It was so strong that night. I cried out, *Mom? Is that you?* I felt her hand on my back. She led me back to Dad. I heard her whisper, 'We miss each other. It's okay, baby. It's what we want. He's not happy.'" She stared into space.

Dad, in a soft voice, brought her focus back. "Did your mom ask you to shoot your dad?"

"I guess. I mean, I really felt he was unhappy. I know ecstasy makes you feel like an empath, but I felt connected with his heart. It's what they wanted. Dad never got over Mom."

"So you shot him?" Susan asked.

"I called Rob to hear his voice. I knew it would ground me. When he answered, I knew I had to do it. It was a win-win. I loved Rob. Dad hadn't changed the will and Rob wouldn't be cut off. He could be with Mom again. You see that, right? My shooting my father was the best thing for all of us."

Susan and Dad exchanged glances.

"I see, I understand, but I've got to place you under arrest for murder," Dad said.

Maxine crossed her arms on the table and lowered her head. She looked around the room. "They're gone." This time she grabbed tissues from the box and sobbed uncontrollably. It was like a weight had been lifted off her.

Dad helped her to stand. "Please stand and place your hands behind your back."

She did as instructed.

Chapter 34

I was late getting to the Legacy. Everyone was already there and the celebration was in full swing. Rita was singing karaoke, and Dad was raising his glass, cheering her on. It didn't seem right to invite Rob and Sharon, even though, in my mind, it was a celebration for him as well. I kept my promise. Extreme emotional disturbance was a defense for murder. We had the psychological examination and documented ecstasy abuse to help persuade the DA to offer the lessor charge.

Maxine agreed to plead to a reduced charge of manslaughter with a six-year sentence. It turned out she had a history of ecstasy and alcohol abuse which was a mitigating factor. Several years before the murder, she had checked into a rehab center under an alias on more than one occasion. She cleaned up a few years after the murder, as it turned out with the same program Rob used. Abuse of ecstasy can cause hallucinations, but I knew Maxine's mom was there that night. I didn't see her, but James said when he left his body she held out her hand, ready to help him cross over. As far as the DA was concerned, she hallucinated, due to excessive and repeated drug use. Drug addiction is deemed a mitigating factor because repeated abuse changes the brain and, over time, rational thinking. Rob was, of course, ecstatic that Maxine wasn't serving life. Still, it didn't seem right that he would be in a room full of people toasting to his sister's arrest.

Nick saw me and started clapping. "Can I get a Whoop! Whoop! for the guest of honor?"

Everyone raised their glass and hollered, "Whoop! Whoop!"

I looked at Dad, nervous that he would feel left out. His glass was raised, and he gave out a 'Whoop Whoop' like he was howling at the moon. Clearly not dejected that I was standing in the limelight.

It was odd to feel joy at both an arrest and a reduced charge. Before Maxine, I hated when a reduced charge was given due to some loophole an attorney found. All my work wasted. Now, I embraced it. There was nothing premeditated about the murder. Maxine didn't bring a gun to the scene like a robber who accidentally shoots someone in the commission of a crime. There was no intent to cause harm when she went home. These factors helped with the manslaughter charge. I raised my glass to Dad and motioned to an open booth. He nodded and followed me.

"How are you feeling, Dad?"

"Like a million bucks. Best retirement present ever."

I wanted to make sure he was over feeling like Maxine had pulled the wool over his eyes. "I talked to Rob; he's been by to see Maxine every day. She was so afraid he wouldn't forgive her. I think they are in a healing place."

"He really turned his life around. I know he will help Maxine when she gets out. Wait, does that mean Rob has to run the business again? He just broke free of all that."

"He's still free. They figured out the best person on the staff to keep things running. Rob's going to check in occasionally, but not enough to interfere with his new career of writing."

"Really! Did he say what his first novel would be about?"

"His journey to recovery."

"He's going to help a lot of people."

"That he is."

"What about you? Are you ready for your next career?"

"I am. My pity party is over. I may not have solved this case but my daughter did, and that is something to be proud of. My legacy isn't just my closing ratio. It's my flesh and blood following in my footsteps, then taking a path in an entirely new direction and setting a new course for advocating for the dead. Not just following the clues, but working hand-in-hand with the deceased victims."

"I can't say this was hand-in-hand with James. He fought me most of the way. But that's my goal, to work directly with the victims to bring their killers to justice."

"I'm behind you. I'll do whatever it takes to keep the lights on in the agency while you and Vicky get the psychic investigations going. I'll take pictures of cheating spouses, underage drinkers, insurance fraud, whatever it takes."

"I appreciate that, Dad. Remember, Sam's going to reach out to have you assist with investigations for the DA. You won't be bored, I promise. Your support means more to me than you know."

"Can I get you a beer?"

"Just one. I've got a big day tomorrow."

"In my day, I'd be nursing a hangover after a big win. What's your big day?"

"It's an experiment. Seeing how healing it was for Rob to get a message from James and how you and Mom connected and forgave each other, I thought I'd set up an opportunity for more people to have that experience. My first winner at channeling a loved one is tomorrow. I want to be fully present to enjoy it. I plan on getting a good night's sleep to enjoy every minute of it. If it's successful, I'm hoping to end every case by channeling a loved one and providing an opportunity for closure or experiencing a defining moment. I would have given anything to see Mom at my wedding. I know I'm not alone in that."

"I'll never get that image of you stopping Rose from ending her life. I'll... I'll never be able to thank you for letting me connect with your mom again. I feel like a weight has been lifted off me. I can't describe what replaced the weight. Joy? Love? A blanket of love and warmth. Something... something wonderful. I think it's a great idea."

"I didn't stop Rose. Her Oma did," I reminded him.

"You know what I mean. You did bring Mom home to me. You can't deny that."

"Yes, she had a face-to-face, but you know she is always with you. Right?"

"I do, even more so now, thanks to you."

Chapter 35

I waited in the foyer for Jennifer's wedding march to start. I saw a picture of her father, Jeff, on the easel near the altar. As far as the guests were concerned, an old friend of her father was going to walk her down the aisle. Only Jennifer and her husband John knew Vicky's coworker Steve would host Jeff's soul for the ceremony.

Jeff cleared his throat a little too loudly and it echoed across the room. I was lost in thought about Mom not being at my wedding or almost wedding and could only imagine it was his second or third attempt at getting my attention. I gave him my best smile. Jeff's soul was fully integrated into Steve's body and he looked a bit unsettled.

"The first time is the hardest."

"Am I supposed to feel like I'm spinning?" he asked.

"I'm sorry, we should have given you a day to acclimate. For me, it's more of a falling forward, tumbling sensation rather than spinning. It's different for everyone. It goes away," I added, hoping to put him at ease.

"Hold your pinky with your thumb. It will help ground you."

"It's working. Thanks." He seemed relieved but nervous.

"You okay?" I asked.

"Yes, I know you told me I was going to be channeled. I just didn't think it would feel this solid. From the movies I've seen, it seemed like only the voice came through. I had no idea that I would be standing here looking out the eyes of someone else, but feeling my heart burst with pride as surely as if I were alive." His voice trembled with emotion.

"Our process is much more than channeling. You fully integrate into the body. In fact, my partner's tagline is '*This isn't your mother's channeling.*'"

Jeff laughed and his shoulders relaxed.

"I'm so glad to be here, to share this moment with my angel."

His voice trembled when he said "angel." He looked unsteady. His face was pale and beads of sweat formed across his forehead. I wondered if Steve's body had a propensity to vomit when he was nervous. I stepped closer, hoping that wasn't the case, and grabbed his arm.

"Are you all right?"

"I always called her my little angel and now I'm her angel. Sometimes she talks to me, and I hear her when she bends God's ear about her troubles. I try to leave her signs that let her know I'm watching over her. Do you think she knows?"

I pulled out a letter from my purse. "She knows. It's one of the reasons I was drawn to her letter."

He looked at the paper, then back at me.

"Shall I read it or would you like to?" I asked, handing it to him.

He didn't take it. "Please read it," he said.

I cleared my throat and read:

Ms. Hanson,

Thank you for the opportunity to see my dad. I hope that you find my story compelling and I am selected in your contest. I'm not the first little girl to dream of her wedding day and her dad walking them down the aisle. My dream died the day my dad collapsed of a heart attack on our front porch when I was twelve. When I heard about your lottery of channeling a loved one for a special event, I got down on my knees and prayed you could help me see my father one last time.

I never got to say good-bye. Being a typical teen, I left for the movies in a huff, angry at my dad for making me change my skirt. I

told him I hated him, called him an
old fart, and told him he was ruining
my life. He was my life. He was
everything and the last words he
heard from me was how much I
hated him. Those last words haunt
me to this day.

I want him to walk me down the
aisle but, more than anything, I
want him to hold me in his arms one
last time. Like most girls, I planned
my wedding day down to the father-
and-daughter dance. Don't get me
wrong, Ms. Hanson, I know he'll be
with me in spirit. I feel him every
day. I connect with him in dreams.
I'll not be alone on my wedding day,
of that I am certain. His spirit
surrounds me. But I need more.
With your team's help, I can have
my father's arms around me for that
one last waltz. We practiced as long
as I can remember. First, me
balancing on his shoes, and later we
twirled around the room like we had
danced for several life times. I just
want to dance in his arms one last
time and let the last words he hears
be how much I love him and miss
him.

I folded the letter and put it back in my purse.

Jeff was crying. "I do visit her in dreams. I didn't realize
she knew I was watching over her. I was hopeful but I wasn't
sure. It breaks my heart she let those words weigh her down
all these years. I forgave her the moment after she uttered
them. She was a young girl struggling to fit in. I just couldn't

let her go out in such a short skirt. I knew she would understand one day."

We turned to face the commotion in the foyer. Jennifer had arrived and there was a flurry of activity. Bridesmaids were arranging her dress; the maid of honor barked orders. "Places, everyone."

The photographer moved to the front to capture everything for posterity.

Jennifer looked beautiful. Her dress was the perfect mix of glamor and glitz, with a bodice filled with white beaded rhinestones. The waist had a mix of sequins and iridescent beads atop a long flowing skirt.

"Are you ready to walk your daughter down the aisle?" I asked Jeff as I straightened his tie.

Jennifer's smile brightened at the sight of him. She held out her hand.

"You're on." I patted his shoulder.

Jeff walked forward and placed Jennifer's arm in his. The wedding march began.

I watched them walk down the aisle. When Jeff gave Jennifer away and she took her place next to her husband John, my throat tightened. I tried to focus on the ceremony, but I couldn't stop thinking of Sam and the vows we wrote for each other. Vows no one would ever hear. Would my life be different now if Mom hadn't died? Would I have felt more grounded on my wedding day? Would my heart have been filled with love and confidence about the life ahead as I waited for my wedding march, instead of doubts?

Had Mom been there to offer words of wisdom, comfort, and reason, would I have run from the church? Would I have abandoned Sam, waiting for me to walk down the aisle? Innocent Sam blindsided on what should have been one of the happiest days. How he found the grace to forgive me, I'll never know.

The room filled with laughter. Jennifer smacked John on the arm. He must have said something funny.

The priest laughed as well and said, "On that note, you may kiss the bride."

Crap, I wasn't paying attention and the ceremony was almost over. I needed to prep for Phase Two. I wanted to make sure everything played out the way Jennifer wanted. The father-daughter dance would be the moment she would cherish above all else. I made my way to the reception where the band was warming up. I asked them to play "Daddy's Angel."

Almost as if on cue, Jeff and Jennifer held hands and walked onto the dance floor.

"You'll always be my little angel," he whispered in a voice thick with emotion. He held up one hand and placed the other around her waist.

Jennifer's eyes brimmed with tears as she took her place in his arms.

I watched in amazement. True to her letter, they floated around the room like they had been dancing through eternity. I looked around the room; most were smiling, a few were crying. I felt the longing from the guests that it should be her father holding her and not his friend. I felt bad they were in the dark. It was too complex to share the truth. I hoped that one day it would be commonplace to stream a loved one.

The song ended. Jennifer told Jeff she loved him and missed him. Her wish had been fulfilled. I let the tears fall freely. Not just at their last dance. I knew Steve had to take the train back, and Jeff would have to return to heaven tonight. My emotions were all over the place. I was sad Mom had passed way before her time. I was grateful to Steve for volunteering his body and proud of my agency for being a part of bringing this wonderful gift. Jeff handed Jennifer to John and walked off the floor.

He was smiling from ear to ear, and he continued to waltz as he made his way to my table. His smile dropped when he saw my tear-stained face. I tapped my watch and reality set in.

He sat down next to me and placed his hand on mine. "Thank you for this. I can't thank you enough. Bless you for doing this, bless this body, bless Steve. I wish I had more time. I didn't think about the good-bye until I saw your face."

"Are you sorry you came?" I asked.

"No. I'm not sure how to say good-bye. I always knew one day I would have to give her away. I'm just struggling with letting her go forever."

The first husband-wife dance was over, and Jennifer and John walked up to the table.

"You're saying good-bye already? Why can't you stay?" she cried. "How can I lose you twice? I'm not ready; don't go."

Jeff stood up and hugged her. "I have to go, Angel; my visit here is over. You may not be able to hold me in your arms after tonight, but I know you always hold me in your heart. I feel your love for me. I hear you when you talk to me. Like when you said, 'Dad, I've got your favorite bandanna stuffed in the front of my dress for something borrowed.'"

She stepped back and laughed as she pulled out a blue bandanna.

"It's something borrowed and blue. A two-for-one."

She laughed as she used it to dry her tears.

"Hon, I'm with you every step of your new life." He took her hand and placed it in John's. "He's got you now."

John wrapped her in his arms. "I'll love her until the day I die. I promise you," he said.

"I'll be watching you. You take care of my girl, or I'll put the haunt on you." Jeff laughed when he said it, but I had a feeling there was truth in those words.

"Can you stay for the toast?" John asked.

Jennifer's eyes widened. "You can, can't you?"

Jeff looked at me. I nodded.

"I wouldn't miss it," he said.

Jennifer and John made their way to the head table.

The best man grabbed a knife from the table and tapped his glass, quieting the room.

"You're going to need one of these." I could feel Nick's breath on my ear as he leaned in to hand me a champagne glass.

I took the glass and stepped back. It was unnerving how close he was. "What are you doing here? Crash weddings much?"

"I didn't crash. I'm your plus one."

"My what?"

"Vicky put me down as your date. I thought you might want some company."

"Oh, you and Vicky thought I was going to be reminded of my wedding and lose it."

"Please don't be mad. She wanted to make sure you're okay. I mean we wanted to make sure. The truth is, I wanted to make sure."

"I'm not mad. I appreciate your concern and hers. Have you been here the entire time?"

"Yes, I stayed out of sight. I didn't want to interfere while you were doing your thing."

Laughter and the clinking of glasses filled the room.

Nick tipped his glass to mine. I gently tapped my glass to his. At that moment, a series of memories flashed in my mind. I was wearing a wedding dress and Nick a tuxedo. We were holding champagne glasses and toasting at our wedding. Was this P-Kate's memory? Then I was in a hospital bed holding a baby with Nick leaning over us holding another baby. We were both smiling for a group picture. Then in front of a car, Nick tossed me the keys and told me it was my turn to drive. A boy and girl around five climbed in the back seat, laughing and poking each other. I realized they were twins. P-Kate and her Nick only had one child, a girl! *This wasn't a memory. This was a vision of my future.*

Chapter 36

I arrived at the office a half-hour before the team. The sign on the door still made me smile. *Third Eye, Inc. and below that Walk-In Investigations Hanson & Hanson.* James was the first of many cases we would solve. I was so proud of the team. Everyone worked well together. After Sarah, we decided to end each case with a round table of lessons learned as a team; then vote on the next case. I pulled my necklace from underneath my shirt and placed the pyramid in the table's center. I wanted P-Kate to join in. I promised I would only ask for guidance when I got stuck on a case. I still felt terrible about her getting in trouble when she gave Sarah's case file. I kept my word. With James, P-Kate gave me a few cryptic hints, but we solved it as a team beyond that. I placed the necklace in my right hand and turned the pyramid activating the portal. As the smoke cleared, I saw P-Kate waving.

"Where's the team?" she asked.

"I thought we could catch up before they got here."

"I'm glad you did. Nick and I had a long talk, and we agreed we need to follow the multiverse laws to the letter. His career's taking off. We can't risk another blemish on his record."

"Does this mean I'll never see you again?" My heart dropped.

"We're entangled since you collided with my world. We'll always be connected. There's a small gap between our worlds. You can bridge that gap with the necklace and pyramid but also with meditation. Remember, I told you that you're not pulled into my world when you use it. You're still standing in yours, observing mine. Your vibration increased to the point you can see through the thin veil separating our worlds."

"I feel like my best friend is moving across the country, and I'm never going to see her again."

"I'm going to teach you a mediation that will help our thoughts connect faster than the speed of light. You'll shift from the 3D-world vibration or consciousness to 5D consciousness."

"You mentioned 5D before. To awaken to the high vibration of the 5th dimension and sustain it, I need to eat healthily, meditate, and then think of you, and we connect?"

"Not just us, even more beneficial, you will connect with your higher self. You'll learn your inner truth, your soul's purpose. Your higher self will help you heal your mind, body and spirit. You'll gain inner strength and wisdom that will astound you. In time, you can bend reality and manifest anything your heart desires. You'll shift from the mind set 'seeing is believing' to 'believing is seeing.' I'm so excited for you."

"Do you think I'm ready?"

"I know you are. When you meditate and go still, close your eyes and ask to connect with your higher self or me. This may blow your mind. You can even ask to connect with your future self. We're all one, past, present, and future. There is no limitation."

"Vicky's been teaching me to meditate."

"Great, then you're one step ahead in the process. I'm going to take back the necklace and pyramid."

I placed them both in her outstretched hand.

"Keep the 5D practice up. It's going to work. Trust me." P-Kate smiled. "In the meantime, pay attention to your dreams and look for signs and symbols. I'll still be reaching out. You've got this. Wipe that frown off your face." She turned the pyramid in her hand. Smoke separated us and, when it cleared, she was gone.

I stood in front of the whiteboard, trying to comprehend what just happened when Mike and Vicky walked in.

"What's up, Boss?" he asked.

"P-Kate shifted how we connect with her on future cases. We need to trust our intuition and pay attention to our dreams, the signs and symbols around us." Rita, and Paul walked in right before I started to teach the techniques. I caught them up as they each took a seat.

"You mean I can ask my future self where he caught the bad guy, and I can just go to the same place and time and catch him?" Mike raised an eyebrow.

"I don't think it's that clear. I think you get better at your intuition and trusting your instincts," Vicky said.

"Yeah, that's what P-Kate said."

Dad walked in. "Sorry I'm late." He looked at Paul, confused.

"Oh, my gosh. Sorry, Paul, I forgot to introduce you. Paul is the one I was telling you had mad IT skills. He helped crack our case when he found photos of Maxine wearing her mom's jewelry. He's joining the team to help out when he can. Our special projects give the program he's working on a good field test."

Paul waved at the team.

A chorus of "Welcome aboard," rang out.

I laughed. "We're definitely in sync with each other."

"Thanks for the warm welcome. I can't wait to work on the next case. If I'm needed."

Dad reached over and shook Paul's hand. "I think we can use you on the next case."

"Um, Dad, we haven't picked the next case. We were going to go through some cold cases we got from the captain."

"Look, I know I jumped to the head of the line when you guys worked on the Baxter case. I can't thank you enough. That was one heck of a retirement present. I'd like to stay ahead of the line here with the next one if you agree. I just got my first case as a private-eye from the DAs office and I think it could use some of the team's magic."

"Sam gave you a case already. That's awesome."

"Don't celebrate. It's a doozy."

"Let's hear it," Vicky said.

"I'm ready for a doozy. I felt like a babysitter on this case. No offense Katie, but you had me running full steam with Sarah. I kinda expected that to be the norm," Mike said.

"No offense taken," I said.

"Okay, Dad, spill it. We're all ears."

Made in the USA
Middletown, DE
20 June 2021